Adam & Noah and the Cops

Adam & Noah and the Cops

Ann Sharpless Bond

Illustrated by Leonard Shortall

Houghton Mifflin Company·Boston·1983

Library of Congress Cataloging in Publication Data

Bond, Ann Sharpless.
   Adam & Noah and the cops.

   Summary: Adventure and mystery find Adam and Noah
when they become involved with a stolen boat, drug
smugglers, a runaway horse, and a woman about to give
birth on the top of a twenty-story building with a
broken elevator.
   [1. Mystery and detective stories. 2. Adventure and
adventurers — Fiction] I. Shortall, Leonard W., ill.
II. Title. III. Title: Adam and Noah and the cops.
PZ7.B6366Ad   1983   [Fic]   82-21181
ISBN 0-395-33225-7

Printed in the United States of America

V 10 9 8 7 6 5 4 3 2 1

For Joshua

CONTENTS

Adam & Noah
and the Cops

1. The Sea Gull

Adam and Noah sat in their rowboat, the Ark, which was tied to the Nelson Warehouse dock.

"Now that school is over, we have all summer to explore this old river," Adam said.

"Sure." Noah stored their lunch boxes under the back seat. "Let's shove off."

"Put on your life jacket," Adam said, buckling his. "You know we promised."

"I don't see why we need them," Noah grumbled. "We're good swimmers."

"Dan helped us fix up this old tub and we agreed to wear life jackets or stay on shore. Isn't that right, Dan?" Adam called to a man shifting barrels at the end of the wharf.

Dan grunted.

Noah buckled on his orange jacket.

"Company coming." Dan stopped rolling a barrel away from the end of the wharf and looked down the river.

The boys looked up and saw a thirty-foot motor-boat heading right for the old wharf. They climbed out of the Ark and stood with Dan watching it.

"Wow," said Adam. "That's a real yacht!"

"It's got a cabin and a brass rail," Noah said with wonder, "and fishing poles sticking up in holders at the back!"

"Sea Gull," Adam read on the bow.

"This is a working wharf." Dan shifted a wad of tobacco in his mouth. "No call for sporting folk to come here."

When the boat drew closer they saw that there were two men in it.

"Too fast." Dan raised both hands in front of him and then lowered them slowly.

At the last moment the boat turned, its side slamming into the end of the wharf. Noah ran over and caught the rope that was thrown to him by the man who had been steering. Adam sat down on the edge of the wharf and used his feet to keep the boat from rubbing against the boards.

A middle-aged man in jeans, a dark blue shirt, and a white cap that read CAPTAIN jumped ashore.

"Tie it up," he ordered Noah. "Keep your feet away from my boat," he snapped at Adam.

Adam perched on a barrel and looked at the Sea Gull. Noah wound a couple of half hitches around a post and joined him.

There was a small deck in front of the cabin. Just inside the cabin a man sat in one of the two seats.

"I need gas," the man in the white cap said to Dan.

"Don't sell gas." Dan spat into the river, just missing the bow of the Sea Gull.

"You can't tell me you don't have any gas." The man was angry.

"Don't sell gas," Dan repeated.

"Bogey!" the man in the boat called.

Bogey went over and stuck his head into the cabin. In a minute he was back. He was smiling, but Adam could tell that he didn't mean it.

"That's my boss," he said to Dan. "He has an important meeting and we're almost out of gas. Maybe you have a can of gas around. I'll pay well for it."

"Gas pump upriver half mile," Dan said.

"We might not get that far," Bogey protested. "Rule of the sea says always help out a ship in distress, right?"

Dan looked thoughtfully at the Sea Gull, then at the boys. Adam was bigger than Noah even though they were the same age.

"Adam," he said finally, "there's a five-gallon can just inside the warehouse door."

Adam got off the barrel and ran down the wharf.

"Have you been fishing?" Noah asked Bogey.

"Sure, fishing," he said.

"Catch anything?"

Bogey laughed. "Good haul, kid, a good haul."

Adam came back slowly with the heavy can.

"I'll go aboard and pour it in for you," he offered.

"No one gets on my boat," Bogey said. He handed the can in to his boss and pulled out a wad of bills.

"Three dollars," Dan said.

Bogey paid him and then held out a five-dollar bill. "This is for your trouble."

Dan shifted the bulge in his cheek and spat even closer to the Sea Gull.

"Don't want your money." He put his hands in his pockets.

No one spoke until the gasoline was poured into the tank, the can was tossed back to Adam, and the Sea Gull had taken off at top speed, heading up the river.

"Too fast," Dan said. "Wastes gas, overheats motor."

"I'm glad that's the last of Bogey," Noah said. "He was mean."

"Why did you let him have that gas?" Adam asked Dan.

"Well, rules of the sea do go for rivers. Wanted to see the last of them, too."

Adam and Noah climbed back into the Ark. It seemed pretty small after the Sea Gull.

"Not too far upstream," Dan called. "Tide change coming."

Soon they were rowing easily toward the middle of the wide river. They sat together on the center seat and each pulled an oar with both hands. Looking downstream at the bridge that barred the big ships from coming up the river, they rested and then waved to the now small figure of Dan on the wharf.

"It would be fun to go under the bridge and row around the big ships." Noah looked longingly at the bridge.

"Sure it would," Adam said, "but we promised not to go under the bridge. There's too much traffic. Dan says not until we're thirteen."

"Three years is a long time to wait." Noah sighed.

"Let's explore the other bank farther up the river. We've never been over there," Adam said. "One, two, stroke, stroke." They swung the boat around and headed upstream.

The sun was bright, the water calm, and they pulled their oars in long, low strokes. They rested when they came opposite the River Sailing Club dock.

The faint hoot of a horn came from the other side of the river.

"There's a boat over there," Adam said. "I wonder why it's hooting. There aren't any other boats around."

"It looks like the Sea Gull," Noah said. "What's it doing? There aren't any docks on that side, just marshy land."

"We were going to that side anyway to explore. Maybe we can find out."

"I didn't like Bogey or his boss," Noah said. "Don't let's get mixed up with them again."

"Mixed up? How can we get mixed up with them?" Adam asked. "We're just going across to look around. We won't even wave to them."

The river was wide here and it took a while for the boys to get near enough to be sure that it was the Sea Gull.

"It's not moving," Adam said. "At least its engine isn't going. It's just drifting. It can't be out of gas."

"It's not hooting at us, is it?" Noah looked all around the river. "There isn't another boat in sight."

"It does look as if it's hooting at us," Adam said uneasily.

"Let it hoot all it wants to," Noah said. "That Bogey didn't even thank me for making two good half hitches."

"Or me for lugging that heavy can. I did want to get on the Sea Gull for just a minute, though."

They could see Bogey now, waving them toward the Sea Gull.

"Let's not go," Noah said.

"We might as well get close enough to see what he says," Adam said. "We don't have to do anything for him."

"Hi, boys," Bogey hailed them. "I'm glad to see you two again. Our engine conked out."

Adam and Noah stopped rowing twenty yards away. They didn't say anything.

"Come a little closer," Bogey said. "You can give us a tow."

The boys backwatered a little.

"The Ark's too small to tow you," Adam objected.

"Just a little way." Bogey smiled at them. "There's a little dock in the weeds in back of us."

"I don't see any dock," Noah called.

"Well, it's there all right. It's kind of hidden," Bogey answered. "Come over here and I'll show you."

The boys kept dipping their oars in the water and gently pushing so they wouldn't get closer.

"We're not strong enough to tow the Sea Gull," Noah said.

"We don't have a long rope," Adam put in.

"I've got plenty of rope," Bogey called.

The boys were silent.

"Look," Bogey said. "I'll give you twenty dollars for just a ten-minute tow."

"We don't want your money." Noah spat over the side of the Ark. Or he tried to; a wet blob ran down inside the boat.

"Noah!" Adam whispered. "What are you saying! Twenty dollars! How can you say we don't want twenty dollars!"

"We shouldn't take his money," Noah whispered back. "Dan didn't."

"What *do* you want?" Bogey was getting angry.

"We want a ride on the Sea Gull!"

"Adam, you said we wouldn't get mixed up with them!" Noah protested.

"Well, we can't let the Sea Gull drift around and get hurt, can we? It's a nice boat. And Dan said the rule of the sea went for rivers too. What do you say to that?"

"I don't like it. That Bogey means trouble."

"I don't like your saying that we don't want twenty dollars."

Bogey had gone into the cabin to talk to his boss. He came out again and called, "OK, we'll row. You don't look very strong at that. I'll get a rope."

Noah still didn't like it, but he was beginning to regret the loss of that twenty dollars. He must learn to spit better, too.

They drew alongside the Sea Gull very carefully so as not to mar the blue paint on the Ark.

Bogey leaned over and yanked each boy onto the deck. He wrapped the end of a long rope around a cleat on the back of the Ark. He had already tied the other end to the bow of the Sea Gull.

The boss was a heavy man. He came out of the cabin and clumsily got into the rowboat without looking at the boys.

The Ark rocked dangerously.

"Be careful with our boat," Adam said. "That's a very good rowboat."

"It's the only boat around, anyway." Bogey rolled up his sleeves and tossed his hat between the two seats in the cabin. "Now, you two sit in there where we can see you, and don't move, understand?"

Noah slid behind the wheel and put his hands on the spokes. Adam sat in the seat beside him.

"Take your hands off that wheel," Bogey ordered. "Don't touch anything! Don't leave these seats, get it?"

His face looked ugly as he loomed over them. Noah took his hands off the wheel and sat on them. Both boys nodded yes. They didn't speak until Bogey had joined his boss and the Ark was slowly moving out in front of them.

"It's no fun if we can't walk around," Adam complained. "I wanted to see the whole boat and those fishing poles."

"I don't see why I can't put my hands on the wheel," Noah said. "I would, too, only those guys are facing us."

The men in the rowboat kept turning around to look for the small dock on the marshy ground. At last, Bogey pointed at the shore and the men began to pull strongly at the oars. The rope tightened and the Sea Gull jerked forward and began to follow the Ark.

"This is no fun at all," Noah grumbled. "I wish we —"

At that moment, the cleat on the Ark that held the rope ripped out of the old wood. It flew up in the air, and rope and cleat snaked into the water. Both men fell over backward, their legs in the air. The boss's oar split in two and the blade end floated away.

"You've broken our oar! See what you've done!" Noah yelled.

"And ripped out our cleat!" Adam was enraged.

Adam went out on the little front deck to call to the men, but as he stood there the Sea Gull swung around, its bow heading downriver. He ran back to the stern deck and was surprised at how small the Ark looked.

"Noah," he called, "come quick!"

"Bogey said we shouldn't move," Noah called back.

"Hurry up!" Adam shouted.

The Ark was getting smaller and smaller. Bogey stood up, waved his arms, and yelled.

"I think he wants us to come back," Noah said.

"Sure he does, but how? The motor doesn't work and the current is taking us down the river."

"Isn't there a brake on this boat?" Noah asked.

"Brake on a motorboat? Don't be silly. Hey! There must be an anchor!"

The minute they thought of an anchor they saw it at once on the deck between the fishing poles. It was fairly heavy, so they both lifted it and heaved it over the stern. They leaned over and watched it splash into the river.

"It won't work," said Noah.

"Why not?" Adam asked. "It's a good anchor."

"There was no rope on it, that's why. We just threw Bogey's anchor into the river and there was no rope on it! He won't like that at all."

"Oh, wow, you're right. I wish you had thought of that before," Adam said.

"I bet he took the rope off it to use for a towrope. He can't blame us for losing his old anchor."

"Look, he broke our oar and pulled out our cleat and just about forced us to get on his boat. Now we're drifting down —" Adam stopped.

Both boys ran to the little deck forward of the cabin.

The river stretched empty ahead of them to the bridge, with only a few buoys here and there. The Sea Gull seemed to be moving a little faster.

"We can forget about Bogey," Adam said. "It's us and the Sea Gull now."

"The tide is out," Noah said. "It's just the current taking us down."

"We're lucky about that. Maybe you can steer us to a buoy and we can tie up on it. I'll get the rope; it's still tied to us."

Adam sat down on the deck and pointed to the nearest buoy. He made the rope into a lasso and practiced swinging it around his head.

"That way," he called to Noah. "No, over there."

He could see Noah swinging the wheel, but it made no difference to the Sea Gull. Sometimes she pointed her bow at the bridge, but mostly she drifted sideways. Once she swung all the way around. But the current always pulled her toward the bridge and the great stone piers that supported it.

Adam jumped up, ran into the cabin, and sat down beside Noah. "She won't steer without her motor going." Adam looked at the instruments in front of him. "If we keep drifting, we'll slam into the bridge and wreck her!"

"Serve Bogey right after what he did to the Ark," Noah said.

"I don't care about Bogey," Adam agreed. "But the Sea Gull is one beautiful ship."

"What about us? We'll be smashed up too! I told you Bogey was trouble. I wish you'd listened . . ."

"We're the crew now. We've got to save the ship!"

There was a key in a lock, a knob that said THROTTLE, and a stick that could be moved backward and forward.

"We need this engine." Adam was grim.

"How do you know it will start? Bogey couldn't do it."

"I don't, but it's our only chance. Maybe it's cooled off enough now."

Adam turned the key. He stood up and looked out the side window. "We're heading broadside at the bridge right now! If the engine starts, steer for the middle of the opening!" He reached for the throttle.

"We're not allowed to go under the bridge!" Noah protested.

"We're not allowed to run a motorboat, either." Adam pulled the throttle. The engine coughed, then caught. He pushed the stick forward a little.

"I can steer now," yelled Noah. He spun the wheel too far one way and then the other. Then he straightened the wheel, and the Sea Gull chugged safely under the bridge.

Adam opened his eyes. "You're some great helmsman!"

"You're some engineer!" Noah said. He steered around a great tanker that lay anchored in the middle of the river. Adam closed his eyes again as they missed a tugboat.

"I guess I'd better turn around and go back under that old bridge," Noah said.

"Not here," Adam said in alarm. "A boat like this needs a lot of space to turn around. Head over to the other side of the river where there aren't any ships or wharfs."

Noah reached down and picked up Bogey's hat from the deck. It said CAPTAIN on it. He put it on his head and shoved it way back so that it wouldn't fall over his face.

"I'll steer going back," Adam decided. He looked at the stick and realized that if he pushed it farther forward the boat would go faster, but with Noah steering it seemed best to leave it where it was.

Slowly they left the busy part of the river and drew near the other shore. Down here the land was marshy too; all the great wharfs were on the opposite bank. It would be a good place to turn around.

When they got near the shore, Noah steered by a big red buoy and swung the wheel to turn the boat. There was a grinding sound underneath and the engine coughed. Adam pushed the stick forward but the Sea Gull didn't respond.

"We've run aground," Adam said. "That red buoy meant that it's too shallow here."

"Why didn't you tell me? You told me to come over here."

"I just found it out," Adam admitted. He turned the key to shut off the motor. "I'm sorry, Noah."

It was very quiet on the Sea Gull for a while.

"The tide will be in soon," Noah said at last. "It will float us off."

"Sure it will! We can explore the boat while we wait," Adam said.

"And Bogey can't stop us. Wow, did those two look funny falling over backward!" Noah laughed so hard the hat fell off.

"Did Bogey ever look mad when he was standing up yelling at us!" Adam started to laugh. "It was all his fault, too!"

"He didn't want you to touch his boat!" Noah whooped.

"I even started his engine when he couldn't!" Adam laughed harder. "It was too hot and just needed a rest. Remember Dan said they shouldn't go so fast?"

"Yeah, he should have known better," Noah said. "We'll take the Sea Gull back to Dan. He'll know what to do."

"Sure," Adam agreed. "Now let's look at those fishing poles."

There were high chairs in back of each pole, and Adam and Noah climbed up on them and pretended to fish for a while. Then they went into the cabin. There were two padded benches running along the walls and a table in the middle.

"This is where they eat, right here," Noah said.

"Sure, and they can sleep on these benches," Adam said.

They found a very small bathroom and a tiny kitchen at the rear of the cabin.

Adam opened the refrigerator, which was tucked under the small sink.

"Something to drink!" He picked up one of the bottles, which were the only things in the refrigerator.

"Oh, beer," he said. "My dad let me taste beer once. It was awful."

"You would think they'd have some soda." Noah rummaged about inside, but there was nothing but beer.

They stretched out on the benches but weren't very comfortable because of their life jackets. The boat slanted toward shore a little as the Sea Gull's keel settled in the mud.

"It's funny that there aren't any fish on board," Noah said. "Bogey said that they had a good haul."

"Did he? I guess you can't trust Bogey. You could tell that Dan didn't like him at all."

"I hope we get the Ark back," Noah said.

They were silent for a while, listening to the water gurgling around the stranded boat.

"If he doesn't give us back our boat," Adam said slowly, "and we keep the Sea Gull, we can take real trips in her. We could bring a lot of food and maybe go all the way down the river and out into the bay."

"I'm not sure I want to go out to the bay. It looks as big as the ocean," Noah objected.

"The Sea Gull could handle the bay! We could chug around for days and anchor at night —"

"We'd have to buy an anchor," Noah interrupted.

Adam laughed. "And a rope! I guess we'll never throw an anchor overboard without a rope again."

The Sea Gull suddenly tipped upright and the gurgling stopped.

"We're floating!" Adam cried, and they dashed forward to the steering wheel. Adam sat behind it and put on Bogey's hat. "You turn the key and pull out the throttle. Then push the stick forward a little."

The propeller churned in the mud for a few seconds and then the Sea Gull was clear. Adam swung the boat in a wide turn and headed for the middle of the river.

"Now, to get back to Dan," Noah said. "And tell him what happened."

Adam glanced down the river toward the bay and sighed.

"OK," he said.

As they chugged slowly and steadily into the

middle of the river, Noah knelt on the seat so that he could see better.

"Watch that tug over there," he said. "Don't get near that big tanker!"

"Look here," Adam objected. "I didn't yell at you when you were steering."

"I'm not yelling," Noah pointed out. "I'm helping. Turn now for the bridge."

Adam carefully swung the bow around.

Noah stood up on the seat and stuck his head out the window. "There's a boat coming up in back of us on your side," he called.

"OK, OK," Adam growled.

"Watch that tug ahead on the right; it's pulling two barges." Noah sat down again.

Adam grunted.

The noise of a motor grew louder through the window on the left. Noah popped his head out the window again and then fell back beside Adam. "It's the Coast Guard patrol!"

Adam tightened his grip and steered straight ahead. They were just passing the tug with the two barges.

The Coast Guard drew very close to the Sea Gull. A man in uniform leaned out the window with a small megaphone and shouted above the noise of the two motors.

"What did he say?" Adam yelled at Noah.

"I think it was 'Heave to.' What does that mean?" Noah yelled back.

The Coast Guard pulled a little ahead of the Sea Gull and began to edge in front of it.

"Slow up," Adam shouted. "Pull the stick!"

Noah grabbed the stick and pushed it forward all the way.

The Sea Gull shot ahead, directly at the patrol boat. Adam swung the wheel hard to the right to avoid it.

As the Sea Gull raced between the two barges behind the tug, the propeller suddenly made a clunking noise. The engine coughed, then resumed its steady whir.

Adam reached over and pulled the stick back. "Pull," he said weakly. "Not push."

Noah stood up again and looked around. "We must have cut the towrope to the last barge; it's adrift," he said. "The Coast Guard has gone to tell the tug. We'd better get back to Dan."

"Yes," said Adam. He felt very tired. "I said pull, not push."

"Oh, did you? With all that noise it was hard to hear. Anyway, maybe it was a good thing. The Coast Guard has left us alone and gone after the tug. Shall I push the stick again?"

"Well, just a little," Adam agreed.

The Sea Gull's speed picked up and Adam began to worry.

"I'm not sure I can land her. She's a lot bigger and heavier than the Ark. We wouldn't want to crash into the wharf after all we've been through."

"Dan wouldn't like that at all," Noah said. "Just bring her in easy."

Adam pushed the hat back, wiped his forehead with a damp hand, and groaned.

"You can do it, Adam." Noah hoped he was right. "Remember to swing around so the side of the Sea Gull comes up nice and gentle against the end of the wharf." Adam looked a bit sick. "Look," Noah went on. "We can do it! I know about this old stick now and I'll just push and pull a little at a time. Dan will help us."

There were no other boats under the bridge and Adam took the Sea Gull right through the middle and swung to the left toward the Nelson Warehouse.

Noah stood up and searched the wharf for Dan. When he didn't see him he hooted the horn. He had wanted to do that for some time. When he popped out again he saw Dan come slowly to the end of the wharf.

Noah waved hard and Dan's hand went up in answer.

Noah fell back in beside Adam. "OK, Captain, take her in!"

Adam licked his lips and pushed back his shoulders. "I'll start a big turn," he said. "You keep pulling that old stick back, but not too fast."

Dan stood at the end of the wharf and made a big, slow circle with his arm. Noah was very careful with the stick, but he couldn't see Dan's signals when he was sitting down, so they were going too fast when they neared the wharf. Dan waved them by.

Next time Adam circled he called out "Slower, slower" when Dan held up his hands and seemed to pat the water. When they were twenty feet away, Dan made a chopping motion.

"Put the stick straight up!" Adam cried.

Noah put the stick in neutral and threw the rope to Dan as the Sea Gull docked gently.

Noah jumped out, but Dan had to give Adam a hand. He wobbled ashore and sat down heavily.

"Nice landing," Dan said. "Did you throw the crew overboard?"

"They took the Ark to pull the Sea Gull," Noah explained.

"They overheated the engine," Adam added, "and it quit."

"Adam got the engine started just in time to keep us from slamming into the bridge," Noah explained.

Dan shook his head and grinned. "But what —" he started to say. Then he glanced out over the water. "More company," he said.

The Coast Guard cutter had shot under the bridge and was heading straight for the wharf at top speed.

They all watched the boat reverse engines and

back to a neat landing at the long side of the wharf. A man in a blue uniform with gold braid jumped out.

"Hello, Dan," he said. "Do you know you're harboring a stolen yacht?"

"Not like me, Mr. Farr." Dan grinned.

"No, it's not." Mr. Farr shifted his gaze to the boys, who were standing close together.

"Know what 'Heave to' means?" he asked.

"We do now," Adam answered. "*Stop*. But we didn't steal this boat. The two men on it made us get on the Sea Gull, and they took our rowboat."

Mr. Farr's eyebrows rose until they almost hit the brim of his cap. He glanced at Dan.

"Two fishy characters brought the Sea Gull in here a while back. Sold them a can of gas. They tried to give me five dollars. Man called Bogey and his boss."

"They said they had caught a lot of fish, but there're no fish on the boat," Noah said.

Mr. Farr turned to his mate, who had a blue uniform too, but not as much gold braid.

"Search her," he ordered. Turning back to the boys, he asked them to tell him about the rowboat.

Adam explained what had happened.

Dan grinned when he heard about Bogey and his boss falling over backward in the rowboat and that Noah wouldn't take their money. He spat angrily into the water, well away from the cutter, when he realized how close the boys had come to crashing into the bridge.

Mr. Farr's mate swung off the Sea Gull.

"Clean as a whistle, sir," he said.

"When did these fishy characters call in here, Dan?" Mr. Farr asked.

"Ten-thirty or thereabouts," Dan answered.

"The Sea Gull was reported missing at six this morning," Mr. Farr said. "Belongs to a Mr. Wallace up the river. Tell me more about where those men wanted to tow their boat." He looked at the boys.

"They talked about a small dock across the river," Adam said. "Almost opposite the Sailing Club, but we didn't see any dock."

"There was a dock there once, sir. It's almost fallen away now," the mate said.

"There must be something on the Sea Gull," Mr. Farr said thoughtfully.

"Only beer," Noah said. "We looked."

"Bring me a beer!" Mr. Farr ordered.

In a minute the mate was back with a bottle. Mr. Farr took a fancy knife out of his pocket and selected a bottle opener. He flipped off the top and tipped the bottle over his hand. White powder poured out.

"That's it," he said with satisfaction. "We got it and now we'll get them."

"What is it?" Noah asked.

"Dope. They were smuggling it. They must have stolen the Sea Gull last night and met a ship in the bay."

"Knew those two were no good," Dan said. "Hope you get them."

Mr. Farr's mate was scanning the river with binoculars.

"Won't be hard, sir," he said. "Two men in a blue rowboat with one oar out there."

"They broke the other one," Noah pointed out.

"I think that Mr. Wallace will be glad to buy you a new one," Mr. Farr said.

"They ripped out our cleat, too," Adam said.

"Got some old cleats around here," Dan put in.

"I think Wallace might pay you to put it on for them," Mr. Farr said.

"Don't want money for that either."

Noah watched carefully as Dan spat. He'd have to practice hard so as not to dribble next time.

"I'm sorry about cutting the barge's towrope," Adam said.

"I guess it was my fault," Noah confessed. "I mixed up pull and push."

"Well, the tugboat captain was mad, but we rescued his barge for him." Mr. Farr got on the cutter. "We'll bring the rowboat back here and my mate will take the Sea Gull to Mr. Wallace after we unload that beer."

"How do you get to be a Coast Guard captain?" Noah asked him.

"Well, it's a little early to be thinking of that, but you've made a start. You've recovered a stolen boat, you've refused a bribe, and you've helped to break up a dope-smuggling ring."

The mate started the engine and the cutter took off after the rowboat. Mr. Farr saluted the three on shore and they saluted back.

Adam's legs were still weak and he sat down on the wharf to wait. "You were right. Bogey *was* trouble," he said. "We should have just left him hooting."

"Steering was fun and so was going under the bridge. I'm glad we had the trip."

"You didn't even want to get on the Sea Gull!"

"I was scared something awful would happen."

"It *did*." Adam grinned and punched Noah's shoulder in a friendly way.

2. The Picnic

Noah zoomed around the corner and braked to a sharp stop in front of Adam's house, bumping into the curb.

"Be careful!" Adam ran down the steps. "I paid for half of that bike, you know!"

"I just saw the girls heading to the park for a picnic," Noah said. "I thought we could follow them."

"Even you can't be hungry yet," Adam objected. "It's only ten o'clock."

"I'm not, but I'd like to see what they've got with them, anyway. Anne and Mary Ellen just had little brown bags, but Bootsy had a *real* picnic basket."

"Maybe she's going to her grandmother's house." Adam was scornful. "You've pedaled for two blocks. It's my turn now."

"OK, but we change halfway to the park." Noah swung off the bike.

"I don't see why you want to chase girls all of a sudden," Adam said.

"Well, I know you like Anne. *I* wonder what Bootsy put in that basket. I bet Anne and Mary Ellen just have plain old peanut butter sandwiches in their bags." Noah got on the back of the bike and hung on to Adam as they took off.

"It's pretty early to start out for a picnic," Adam said. "What part of the park were they headed for?"

"That's just it! They wouldn't tell me. They just said it was their hideaway. I bet we could find it."

"What will we do if we *do* find them?" asked Adam. "Scare them?"

"Sure," Noah agreed. "They must be hidden somewhere, and we could sneak up —"

"And be wolves after Little Red Riding Hood and her basket!" Adam finished.

Both boys laughed so hard the bicycle wobbled dangerously. They practiced howling like wolves the rest of the four blocks to the park, and Noah forgot to remind Adam that it was his turn to pedal. They changed places at the park.

Noah found pedaling over grass, particularly bumpy grass, a lot harder than he expected. After a little way he stopped.

"It's your turn," he said.

"You haven't been pedaling two blocks," Adam objected.

"But you're bigger and stronger than I am."

Adam was pleased that Noah admitted this, so he pushed hard and got them down to the long stretch of grass where mothers played with their little kids. The girls were nowhere in sight.

After this they rode some and pushed some as they circled the big open space.

"This is no fun," Adam protested. "We can't find them. Let's go."

Noah began to howl again, and Adam laughed and joined in.

"Look," Adam said, "there couldn't be a secret place out in the open like this. It must be way over there in the woods."

"Sure, Red Riding Hood went through the woods."

"And in the woods there's a path where people ride horses," Adam said. "That would be just right for a bike."

They pushed the bike toward the woods until they came to where the ground dropped away in a long slope.

"Good," Adam said. "We can coast the rest of the way."

They climbed on the bike and shot down the hill, howling as they went. When they came to a stop at the bottom, there were tall trees and a lot of underbrush ahead of them.

"I know there is a path through here some-where." Adam looked around.

They pushed the bike for quite a while along the edge of the trees but found no path.

"I guess we should have walked in the other direction." Adam stopped and sat down to rest.

"It's a long way back," Noah pointed out, "and we don't want to be late. I bet we could get this old bike through the bushes right here."

"Late for what?" Adam asked. "After we scare them you don't think we'll get any of the picnic, do you?"

"Well, we don't need to scare them very much. Let's try. That path for horses can't be very far on the other side of this stuff."

They had a terrible time with the bike. Every bush and bramble caught at the spokes in the wheels. It seemed very heavy as they lifted and pulled and dragged it along. At last they came to the bridle path and flopped on the ground.

"That's a pretty high bank on the other side of the path," Adam remarked. "We never would have gotten this old bike over that."

"Those are good rocks to climb on, though," Noah said. "Say, I bet the girls' hideaway is over there somewhere!"

"Sure it is," Adam agreed. "We can just ride along first in one direction and then the other until we find them."

They started out toward the left with Noah pedaling. Adam hung on the back and thought about

31

Anne. After they found the girls and Noah had gotten off, he might show her how he could ride with no hands. They rounded a bend in the path and Adam gave a happy wolf call.

Noah braked to a stop. Three girls were sitting on a grassy patch in front of a rocky cliff.

Bootsy jumped up, her pigtails flapping. "Hey, you've been following us!"

"It's a free park," Adam said. "I thought you had a hideaway."

"So you thought you'd find it? We haven't gone there yet."

"Why were you hollering?" Mary Ellen asked. "Were you scared, Adam?"

Adam didn't answer. He looked at Anne. She had a skirt on — not jeans like the others. Her yellow hair shone in the sun.

Just then a faint clippity-clop sound could be heard around the bend. Anne stood up and Noah pushed the old bike off the path. A horse and rider came into sight.

"Man oh man, look at that horse," Noah murmured.

"And the rider," Anne whispered.

The rider, a tall young man, raised his crop in a little salute and smiled at Anne as he rode by.

"Wow, did you see that horse!" Bootsy said. "That was a thoroughbred, I bet!"

"Sure it was. Did you see the way it picked its

feet up high and its neck arched a little?" Noah shook his head in wonder.

"That rider is one handsome man," Mary Ellen sighed.

"He knows how to ride," Anne said. "He kept his heels down, his back straight, and he held the reins low."

"I guess anyone could ride if he had a horse," Adam said.

"You need special clothes," Mary Ellen said. "He had those riding pants and coat, and one of those funny black hats."

"I wouldn't need those clothes," Bootsy put in. "Cowboys ride in jeans!"

"You couldn't ride," Noah jeered. "You're too small!"

"Not much smaller than you are!"

Adam gave up the idea of showing how he could ride the bike with no hands.

"You're lucky, Anne. He smiled at you," Mary Ellen said. "He didn't even *look* at me."

"I'm going to take riding lessons in the fall." Anne smiled dreamily. "Maybe I'll meet him riding along here someday."

Adam kicked back the bike stand and swung into the saddle. "Come on, Noah," he said. "Let's not hang around here anymore."

"What's the hurry?" Noah asked, but he climbed on back.

"Girls!" muttered Adam as he pedaled away fast

in the same direction as the horse and rider. "What do you want to waste your time with them for?"

Noah hadn't been ready to leave. He hadn't even found out what was in Bootsy's picnic basket, but he could tell that Adam was mad about something. He was standing on the pedals and going very fast. Noah held on tight to the seat and yowled with all his might.

Adam kept up his pace for a long time. Noah was surprised because going that fast was hard work. Suddenly, around Adam, Noah got a glimpse of a sharp turn in the path. His howl turned into a scared yell when the bike tipped dangerously as they rounded the curve and then straightened up. The horse and rider were trotting straight at them.

The horse, startled by the fast-moving bike, twisted away from it and reared straight up on its hind legs. The rider slid off the saddle onto the path. Adam jerked the handlebars and just missed running over him. The horse bolted off in the direction of the girls.

"Stop!" Noah cried.

When Adam had slowed up, he turned the bike around and rode back by the fallen rider.

The man struggled to a sitting position.

"You kids almost killed me!" he yelled. "You have no —"

Seeing that the rider was unhurt, Adam pedaled

faster and they were back around the bend again before Noah could object.

"You almost killed us too!" Noah cried angrily. "We should have stopped. Maybe that guy was really hurt."

"We're going after the horse."

"But you can't just leave him there!"

"We'll tell Mary Ellen. She thinks he's so wonderful. She can go see if he's OK."

"Adam, you shouldn't have gone around the curve so fast. Look what you've done! Stop going so fast!"

"We're getting help for him, aren't we? And you were yelling, don't forget. That scared the horse too, you know."

Noah couldn't believe that Adam could still stand on the pedals and pump so hard, but he did until they came in sight of the grassy spot where they had met the girls.

Mary Ellen and Anne ran out in the path and waved. Adam was careful to stop well in front of them.

"What happened to the rider?" Anne asked. "His horse just came by here alone."

"He's not such a great rider," Adam said. "He fell off."

"We were charging around a curve," Noah put in. "That horse was galloping along and almost ran into us. He stood up on his hind legs and *whammo!* The man bit the dust!"

"You scared the horse!" Anne cried.

"He almost kicked us!" Adam said. "Say, that rider couldn't even stay on him! *We* didn't fall off."

What they had said was true, Noah thought, but it had seemed a little different at the time. He didn't think the horse had really been galloping, and *they* were the ones who had whizzed around the bend. "I hope that man is not really hurt," he said.

"You don't know?" Mary Ellen cried. "You just left him there on the ground?"

"He could yell," Adam said.

Mary Ellen stuffed the picnic things behind a bush. "I'll rescue him."

"I'll come too," Anne said.

"Where's Bootsy?" Noah called as the girls headed up the path.

"She's gone after the horse," Anne answered.

"I don't see why Anne has to go," Adam grumbled.

Noah knew it was because the young man had smiled at her, but he didn't say so. "Maybe we should help Bootsy catch the horse," he said instead.

"Sure, that's what I wanted to do all along. You pedal for a while."

They changed places and Noah set off at a slow speed. He didn't think Bootsy would catch the horse in a hurry, and he was going to be careful in case it turned around again and headed back toward them.

Soon they caught up to Bootsy jogging slowly along.

"Hi!" she said. "Did you see what happened?"

"Yes," Adam said. "That guy fell off. He's not such a great rider."

Noah pedaled very slowly so that Bootsy could keep up with them.

"He's a good rider, all right. I bet something scared the horse," she said.

The boys were silent.

"I'm going to take his horse back to him," she went on.

"How?" Noah asked.

"I'll decide when I find him."

Adam had a plan of his own, but he decided not to say anything just yet. The bike wobbled because it was going so slowly, and he got off to jog along with Bootsy.

Noah steered circles around them.

"Watch out," Adam warned.

"I bet I know what scared the horse," Bootsy said. "That old bike of yours."

Noah braked. The horse was ahead of them, munching leaves off a bush beside the path.

"I knew he'd stop and eat," Bootsy whispered, "after all that running."

"We'll creep up on him," Adam said.

Bootsy and Adam walked toward the horse very quietly. He didn't seem to notice them at all. Noah wheeled the bike some distance behind.

"You grab the reins," Bootsy said, "and I'll climb up. I want to ride him back. He's nice and calm now."

Adam was shocked. From the moment the rider had fallen off, he had been determined to ride the horse himself. That would be a whole lot better than riding "no hands" on an old bike. He'd show Anne that he could keep his heels down, sit up straight, and hold the reins low. He didn't say anything about that. He needed Bootsy to help catch the horse first.

Noah was glad to hang back with the bike as he watched the other two steal up to the horse. When they were about ten feet away, it jerked up its head and ambled farther down the path. This happened three times.

"I'll circle around," Adam said finally. "I'll creep through the woods and get on the other side of him. He'll come toward you and then you can catch him."

Noah pushed the bike to the very edge of the path and he and Bootsy sat down to wait for the horse to come by.

Adam's plan worked well. By going through the woods, he had managed to get on the other side of the horse and it didn't even look up as he walked slowly toward it.

He hesitated. The horse looked a lot bigger up close; the saddle was a long way from the ground. Then he remembered how he'd planned to ride the bike no hands for Anne. That was before she'd seen the young man on the horse. He *had* to get up onto that saddle.

The stirrups were long. The young man must have much longer legs than he did. But the stirrups hung down far enough so that he felt he might be able to lift his left foot and slip it into one stirrup. Then he could grab the saddle and pull himself up as he swung his other leg over the horse's back. He had seen cowboys do this a hundred times on TV. He thought about sitting up straight and holding the reins low as he trotted by Bootsy and Noah. Then they could ride the bike while he rode the horse back to the girls.

But he was just a little too anxious. He gave a kind of leaping hop on his right leg, with his left leg just as high as he could get it. This didn't get him quite near enough to the stirrup, and he fell heavily. The horse gave a mighty plunge, kicked with its hind legs — missing Adam's head by inches — and took off at a gallop back down the path toward Bootsy and Noah.

"He's coming!" Adam bellowed. "Catch him!"

Bootsy and Noah didn't hear Adam yell. The sound of thudding hoofs drowned out his voice.

"Adam scared him!" Bootsy shouted as the horse came into sight. "We'll have to slow him down!"

Noah grabbed the bike and rolled it across the path. The horse hadn't liked it before, so maybe it would slow him down now.

The horse came at the bike at full gallop. He seemed to bunch himself together, then he sailed over the bike and continued pounding down the bridle path.

Adam came trotting along from the other direction.

"Why didn't you stop him?" he called.

"Why did you get him started so fast?" Bootsy asked. "A brick wall wouldn't have stopped *that* horse."

"He's a great jumper, too," Noah added. "Hey, why do you have dirt all over you?"

"I fell down."

"That must have scared him," Bootsy said. "I knew that was one scared horse."

"A guy can't always help falling down." Adam brushed off his pants.

"I'm not sorry he got away," Noah said. "He's sort of scary when he goes fast."

"I'm not scared of him." Bootsy kicked up the bike stand and wheeled it along. "I want to ride him."

"You couldn't," Adam said as they walked along. "The stirrups are too long and he's a very tall horse. It's going to be hard enough for *me* to get on him."

"Why do you think you can if I can't?" Bootsy demanded. "Just because you're a boy?"

That was just what Adam did think, but he didn't say so.

Bootsy climbed onto the bike and took off. Adam ran after her.

Noah followed slowly. Sure, it would be fun to ride a horse, but he had seen one rider bite the dust and *he* wasn't about to try it. He doubted if either of them could get on in the first place and was sure they wouldn't stay on long even if they did. Pretty soon he caught up to Adam, who was now only walking.

"I don't see why you want to ride," he said.

"You wouldn't," Adam said.

"Just because that guy can ride with his heels down and all that stuff and Anne is going to take riding lessons, why do you —" Noah stopped. That was it. Adam had to show Anne that he could ride as well as anybody. It was silly, of course, but when Adam had to do something he generally did it.

They walked along in silence all the way back to the grassy spot where they'd met the girls. The horse stood on the path, sticking its head deep in a bush by the side of the path. When it raised its head, they saw it was eating a ham sandwich.

"He's found the picnic!" Noah whispered.

The boys watched as Bootsy appeared from behind another bush. She held out an apple and the horse's soft lips scooped it up. She looked up and saw the boys. "I've got him tied up," she said. "I'm calming him down before I get on."

Adam and Noah moved closer and saw the reins looped over the stump of a large tree.

"You've got to help me," Adam whispered to Noah. "Stand on that stump and hand me the reins. I'll get up on the other side of him."

Noah wasn't eager to get that close to the horse, but it looked very peaceful now. He wanted to talk Adam out of his plan, but from the look on Adam's face he knew it wouldn't work. It might be fun to watch Adam ride, at that.

He walked quietly to the stump and got on it as Bootsy fed the animal another apple. Huge teeth munched on a piece of metal as well as the apple. Noah saw Adam on the other side of the horse and wondered how he was going to get into the saddle.

Adam wasn't so anxious this time; after all, the horse was tired. He gave a hop and jump. His foot went into the stirrup and he grabbed the saddle and pulled hard. His other leg swung over the horse's back and he was astride.

Noah unhooked the reins and tried to give them to Adam, but the horse pulled away from the stump and Noah felt himself falling. He grabbed Adam's arm and yelled, and as he did, the horse backed up and snorted. Adam tried to get the reins, but Noah held on tight. As Noah came loose from the stump, Adam clutched Noah's belt and pulled — and Noah ended up face down hanging across the horse's back. Squirming and kicking, he managed to get a leg on each side and found himself, both arms around Adam's waist, riding backward.

Adam had to reach around Noah to find the reins, which Noah had finally dropped. As he felt for them, the horse tossed his head in the air, slid the bit between his teeth, and leaped forward.

To the left of Adam's ear Noah saw Bootsy shaking her fist.

The force of the horse's forward thrust drove Noah's chin hard into Adam's shoulder. "I don't want to be here," he said between clenched teeth.

"Squeeze the horse with your legs," Adam said. "Stop squeezing *me!*"

Noah tried to squeeze with his legs, but he didn't loosen his grip on Adam.

"Why am I riding backward?" he asked.

"Because you got on backward, that's why," Adam said. "If you hadn't gotten on, I bet you could have —"

"I didn't *want* to get on!"

Adam wished he could lean forward over the horse's neck like a jockey, but he doubted that Noah would bend far enough backward.

"Pull the reins and slow him down," Noah begged.

"The reins don't work!" Adam sounded uneasy.

"I bet he's chewing on that metal thing," Noah said. "The reins are hooked on to it. Anne said other stuff about your heels and back or something."

"The stirrups are too long for my legs. They're banging against the horse and I think that's what's keeping him going. And stop pushing me backward." Adam sounded more than uneasy this time.

In galloping, the horse's front legs worked together as did the back ones. The four hoofs almost met under the horse's belly, then the front legs shot forward as the back legs thrust backward with great force. This produced a kind of rocking motion, and pretty soon the boys got used to it.

"I'm not sure how I got on." Noah finally loosened his chin grip on Adam's shoulder. "This old horse was just standing there eating apples. Why didn't you take the reins?"

"You wouldn't let go of them, that's why."

"Maybe he'll stop to eat again. That's what he likes — eating and running."

"He just ate the picnic."

Noah began to wonder if he could get off. He felt that he had showed he could ride a horse, even if he hadn't meant to.

Adam saw a bend in the path a good way ahead

of them. He wondered if it was the one where they had left the rider. If it was, Anne was probably there with Mary Ellen.

He felt he was doing pretty well so far, except for having Noah wound around him like an octopus. He pushed down his heels even though they didn't reach the stirrups, held the reins low, and sat up as straight as he could. Riding wasn't hard once you were used to it. It was almost like being on a merry-go-round.

Gradually the horse slowed. Noah hoped it would stop altogether and let him slide off. His chin ached from digging into Adam's shoulder.

"I think he's about to quit," he said.

Adam grunted.

But the horse had no idea of quitting. He changed his pace to a fast trot. Suddenly the rocking motion was gone. Each of the animal's hoofs seemed to hit the ground at a different time. Even the boys didn't go up and down together. Noah bit his tongue.

They rounded the bend, stirrups flopping, bouncing separately, reins high, Adam's toes digging into the horse's sides in an effort to stay on.

The girls looked surprised. The young man looked angry.

Adam had planned a little salute for Anne, but the man yelled and the horse swerved. Noah let go of Adam and grabbed the saddle. They shot

away at full gallop past the little group, still astride.

"I kept us on," Noah said finally.

"We looked awful," Adam said. "Bouncing along!"

"She was laughing," Noah said. "I saw her over your shoulder."

"Who?"

"You know who."

Adam did know. Anne was laughing at him. After all he'd been through to show he could ride, Anne laughed! He'd ridden, too — not quite the way he'd planned, but he'd stayed on, hadn't he?

When the horse began to slow up, Adam pulled hard at the reins. He couldn't stand to go through that awful trotting business again. For the first time the horse walked.

"Let's get off," Noah said. "Now's our chance before he pulls something else."

Adam wanted to get off too. He thought that maybe they could turn the horse around and it would go back to the young man. Then he and Noah could cut through the woods and head for home. Bootsy would be glad to ride the bike back. He wouldn't have to go by the others at all.

He yanked on the reins again, and when the horse stopped, Noah slid to the ground.

Adam was surprised what a difference it made

not to have Noah in front of him. For the first time he felt like a real rider. The horse was tired, too. That made a lot of difference. He pulled on the left rein and the horse turned around.

"I'll just walk him back," he said. "It's nice up here now."

Noah walked along beside him, but not too close. Adam was able to sit up very straight and, except for his clothes, he thought he looked every bit as good as the young man.

Even the horse seemed relieved to be walking. Noah sang "Home on the Range" as they went along.

Soon they could see the little group ahead. The young man got up and stood in the middle of the path. The boys were pretty sure he would have enough sense not to holler at them again. As they drew near, the girls stood up and watched.

" 'Where never is heard a discouraging word,' " Noah sang.

They were only ten feet away from the young man when Bootsy, on the bike, zoomed around the bend straight at them.

The horse stood on his hind legs. Adam flung his arms around the horse's neck. Noah, behind them, let out a yell. The horse shot his nose almost to the ground, and Adam did a somersault over his head and landed on his feet. He staggered forward, then backward several times.

When he stopped, he put his hand up in a little salute to Anne.

There was dead silence for a second. Then a roar of laughter.

The young man managed to grab the reins, but then he bent double with loud snorts and splutters.

Adam was stunned from landing so hard on his feet but more stunned at the sight of Anne and Mary Ellen. They were laughing so hard they had to hold each other up. Bootsy had fallen off the bike and was rolling around yelping with joy.

Even Noah thought it was very funny.

Adam just stood there while everyone laughed at him.

"You should be in the circus," the young man gasped.

"You'd make a great clown!" Mary Ellen said, and this set them off again.

"I didn't mean to get off *that* way!" Adam said bitterly.

That didn't help. They thought everything was funny.

Noah came over and stood beside Adam. "We had a good ride anyway," he said.

"You sure did," Bootsy agreed. "I would have too, only you tricked me."

"You let the horse eat the picnic," Noah said.

"It was worth it," Mary Ellen giggled. "To see you two bouncing by with Noah backward, then

Adam doing a loop-the-loop over the horse's head and landing on his feet!"

"A good show," the young man said as he mounted and rode off.

"It was just like you, Adam." Anne smiled at him.

Suddenly Adam didn't mind being laughed at. He jumped on the bike and rode no hands around the bend, with Noah howling behind him.

3. The Elevator

"You've ruined the day already," Adam said as he and Noah stood at the bus stop on the corner of Fifty-second and Chestnut streets. It was a very hot day and he was grumpy.

"I don't *want* to go to the old dentist. I *have* to. It won't take long. If you come with me we can go on right to the zoo." Noah paid both fares as they boarded the downtown bus.

"Anyway," Noah went on, "you'll like the elevators. You push the buttons yourself and the building is twenty stories high. I usually take a ride or two first."

Adam was silent. Waiting in a dentist's office was no fun even when you didn't have to see the dentist yourself.

When they swung off the bus at Broad Street Noah pointed to a brand-new building across the street. A sign over the door read DIXON BUILDING.

"Twenty stories is tall, all right," Adam said. "Can we go to the top?"

"My dentist is on the last floor."

Inside the lobby Noah showed Adam the board that listed the names of the tenants. He pointed to one of the names. "There he is — Dr. Cannon, room nineteen-oh-six. That means he's on floor nineteen, room six."

"You said he was on the last floor, that would be two thousand and six."

"That floor hasn't been finished yet. My dentist said they're making an apartment up there for Mr. Dixon. Come on, we've got time for a ride."

Only one elevator was on the ground floor. A man stood near the control buttons, so Noah held Adam back. "No fun unless you can push them yourself," he said.

When the next elevator came down they hurried inside and Noah took charge of the buttons.

"Going up," he sang out. "Call your floors, please!"

Noah pushed all the right buttons as the people called out their floor numbers, and the last passenger got out at floor sixteen. On the way down in the empty elevator they pushed some buttons and stopped, but no one got on. They watched the numbers light up above the door as the elevator passed each floor.

"We'll have to get out at nineteen this time,"

Noah said when they reached the lobby. "You push and I'll call out."

While Noah was saying "Step this way" and "Going up," Adam noticed a blank button above number nineteen. Only one person, a large lady, said nineteen, and Adam pushed the blank button instead. He wanted to go to the very top and he could always push number nineteen later.

The big lady moved toward the door as eighteen flashed by. Noah yelled, "Hey, wait!" as nineteen came and went.

The elevator stopped and the doors slid open. The floor in front of them was covered with tools and cans of paint. A great canvas cover was bunched up in the middle.

"You hit the wrong button," the woman said. "This isn't nineteen."

"Say, this is twenty." Noah stepped out and looked to the right. "There's open roof out there."

Adam joined him. "We made it to the top, all right."

"I want nineteen," the woman said. The boys hopped in as she pushed the button.

The doors stayed open and the elevator didn't move. Noah pushed the button hard, then Adam tried it. Nothing.

"You must have broken it," the woman said. "Now I'll have to walk down."

Adam was disappointed. There certainly hadn't been much to see on floor twenty.

"You two go find the stairs. I guess I can get down them if I have to," the woman said.

The boys went to the left and found a solid door marked STAIRS. They each tried the handle but it wouldn't turn. There was a keyhole below it.

"You couldn't even push the right button!" Noah said.

"Anyone can make a mistake."

"But you did it on purpose. You wanted to come up here all along. And now look at the mess we're in!"

"Look, I didn't want to come to your old dentist in the first place," Adam said angrily. He hung back while Noah told the lady about the stairs.

"I can't stay up here all day," she said.

"There's a bench out here," Adam heard Noah say. "We can take the paint cans off of it."

"The smell of paint makes me sick."

Adam didn't see why of all the people who had ridden the elevator, they should be stuck with this large woman who complained about everything. Finally, though, he helped Noah carry the bench out the door and onto the roof of the nineteenth floor. The twentieth floor was much smaller than the ones below. The elevator shaft rose high above them and gave a little shade. They put the bench there.

"Maybe the workmen are out to lunch," Adam said.

The woman sat down and put her feet up. "They don't work on Saturdays."

Noah sat on the floor in the shade beside the bench and Adam walked around. It was very hot; the sun bounced off the roof and the breeze was light.

Adam began to be very sorry about pushing that blank button. He guessed that people down below would find out the elevator was stuck and fix it, but when? Not in time for the dentist or maybe even the zoo. He hoped he'd hear the doors clang shut when it was fixed.

He stopped to listen and then heard another noise. It was a faint roar from the street below.

He leaned over the four-foot wall that ran around the roof. Far below the traffic was stalled. All along Chestnut Street and up Broad the cars were jammed bumper to bumper. A lot of horns were blowing.

Adam ran to the far corner of the building. The traffic lights at the corners weren't working. He stared at them for some time, hoping to see them flash on.

"Noah!" he yelled. "Come quick!"

"Look what I've done!" he cried when Noah was beside him. "I've caused a power failure!"

Noah looked at the stalled cars and the blank traffic lights.

"You did *that?*"

"Sure. When I pushed the wrong button! All the electrical wires are connected, you know. Noah, please don't tell anyone I did it!"

"There isn't anyone to tell," Noah said. "That lady is going to have a baby. She's not interested in anything else."

"She's what?"

"Didn't you see how big she is? My mother was like that before my brother was born."

"Well, I guess that's why she complains a lot. Don't tell her what I've done. She's mad at me already."

A helicopter flew low over Chestnut Street. "Say, that's the TV station's copter," Noah said when Adam could hear. "I guess this power failure is pretty important."

The boys ran all around the roof looking down at the clogged streets.

"Man, you did a job, all right," Noah said. "The whole city's tied up."

"Look, Noah. I *did* mean to push that blank button. I *did* want to come all the way up. But I *didn't* mean to do all this! You won't tell anyone, ever, will you?"

"Well, no, but you do get us in trouble a lot."

"*I* do? You're crazy! I'm the one who gets us *out* of trouble."

"First *you* get us into it. We *both* get us out of it."

"Just because I pushed one little wrong button you —"

Noah went back to the woman.

Adam walked up and down. He couldn't sit still and it made him feel worse leaning over the wall and seeing all those mad-looking cars down there. He didn't think Noah was right but he decided if he ever got down on the ground again he'd be more careful about doing what he wanted to do.

After a while Noah joined him. "She's doing well," he reported. "She timed the pains with my watch and they are five minutes apart."

"What does that mean?"

"Well, my dad took my mother to the hospital when hers were two minutes apart."

"You mean she's going to have a baby?"

"I told you that already."

"You mean right now?"

"Well, you can't always tell how fast it will be. Sometimes —"

"Noah! She can't have it here! Do something!"

"I'm not a doctor, you know. What can *I* do?"

"Tell her if the helicopter comes back maybe we can get it to take her to the hospital. There's plenty of room for it to land here."

"You tell her. I don't think she wants a ride right now."

"You're the one who knows all about this kind of thing." Adam rubbed his sweating face on his sleeve. "Noah, I don't even want to look at her!"

Noah remembered how Adam disliked hospitals and what went on inside them. He wouldn't even look at some TV programs.

They saw the helicopter circling down by the river.

"I'll tell her later," Noah said. "The chopper might come back any minute. We'd better be ready for it."

They ran into the room in front of the elevator.

"If we could find a rope, one of us could climb down and knock on a window," Adam suggested.

Noah was relieved that all they could find was string. He was sure Adam would have tried to talk him into climbing down because he was lighter.

They found a large can of paint and a wide brush and decided to make a sign on the roof for the helicopter.

"What will we print?" Noah asked. "Baby being born?"

"Too long," Adam said. "S.O.S. is what we should put." He printed the letters as high as he was tall, on the widest part of the flat roof.

Noah put "Help" underneath, just in case the pilot didn't understand S.O.S. He went back to the woman.

Adam shivered when he saw Noah hand her his watch. He searched the sky but there was no sign of the helicopter, so Adam went to the side of the building away from Noah and the woman. He didn't want to hear any more about her pains. Beneath him the windows were closed and a long way down.

Across the street, in a smaller building, people were leaning out of windows. He waved and hollered but they were so far below him that they couldn't hear him. They just waved back.

"Paper airplanes!" he cried. "I'll fly messages down!"

There were a lot of old newspapers near the paint, and he folded them quickly and wrote messages on the wings, using a small brush dipped in black paint. "Help! Get key to stairs, Dixon Bldg.," and "Police — baby due on Dixon roof."

He took them out to show Noah. "Look," he called. "Help is on the way!"

Noah ran over to watch the launching.

The first one sailed beautifully. The light breeze caught it and took it high in the air. They watched it swerve and glide for a long time. Finally it settled on a garage roof across the street.

"Wow, that was some ride," Adam said.

"It didn't help much." Noah launched the next one. It disappeared almost at once beyond some high buildings down the street. "Someone might find it." Noah ran inside to make some more. He came back and started launching them as fast as he could.

"Hey, you don't have messages on some of them," Adam objected.

"Well, I don't think anyone will find them anyway. It's fun, and there's nothing else to do."

"I thought you were taking care of that woman."

"She's taking deep breaths to try and slow things up."

Adam leaned on the wall and looked around at the barely moving city. "I feel funny," he said, "knowing I did all this."

"You wouldn't think it was funny if you were having a baby."

"I don't mean funny, exactly. Kind of powerful."

"Adam! You like it! How can you?"

"I didn't say I like it. Anyway, you like shooting airplanes around without any messages on them."

"That's not the same and you know it!" Noah marched away.

Noah was right, of course, Adam thought. Playing like a little kid with paper airplanes was not like making a whole city stop. That was the kind of thing only Superman did. Or Adam.

He noticed a clock on a building across the street. It gave the time when he must have pushed that blank button. He thought of all the other things that had stopped, too — dentist drills, washing machines, subway trains, doorbells, big machines in factories.

"It's scary," he whispered to himself. "Zappo."

He walked all around the wall, not looking at the woman on the bench as he went by.

"She knew she was going to have a baby," he muttered. "Why didn't she stay home? What if the elevator door hadn't opened and we'd been stuck inside with her? She's gotten us into an awful mess!"

As he walked by her the second time, Noah ran over to him. Adam looked at him in alarm; Noah was excited.

"Four minutes," Noah said. "She said —"

"She should have stayed home!" Adam cried. "She had no business getting stuck on a roof!"

"She said you didn't do it."

"You told her! You promised you'd never tell anyone. What will all those people do to me?"

"Listen, won't you? I didn't tell her. She heard the cars honking and asked me why they were making so much noise. I told her the traffic lights were out and she said it must be a power failure and that's why the elevator wouldn't work."

"But I punched the button."

"Sure you did. But the elevator brought us up here, didn't it? The power went off *after* we got here."

"I thought I made it happen," Adam said slowly.

"That's because you felt guilty."

For a few seconds Adam felt almost sorry that he

hadn't caused the blackout. He had felt guilty, all right, but powerful too.

"It wasn't my fault at all," he said. It was hard to get used to the idea.

"We whizzed by the nineteenth floor," Noah pointed out. "If you'd punched nineteen instead, we wouldn't have been stuck up here with her."

"Is she mad at me?"

"Not any more. She says making that S.O.S. sign was smart. She doesn't want a ride now, but she'll take one, all right."

"That helicopter is our only hope." Adam searched the sky frantically.

"There it is." Noah pointed. It looked like a small speck far across the city.

"I bet it's flying low to take pictures for the evening news. It will be a long time before it gets to us. Say, this building is the highest one around. Maybe we can signal it."

"How?"

"I don't know. Come on." Adam led the way inside.

They searched the unfinished rooms for some time.

"We need a flag and a pole," Noah said. "Then we can wave it back and forth and the pilot will see it."

They searched everywhere but there was nothing they could use for a flag.

"I've got a red shirt on," Noah said. "We can use that."

The nearest thing to a pole was a ladder lying against a wall. Together they could lift it, but it was too heavy for them to hold upright.

"Well, there goes that idea. Anyway, the pilot would probably just think we were drying my shirt." Noah sat down on the crumpled-up canvas in the middle of the room.

Adam stopped in front of a pail. "This is heavy enough to go right down," he said. "I could tie a note to this and drop it over."

"And hit someone on the head?" Noah cried. "Haven't you caused enough trouble already? The sidewalk is *full* of people!"

"I didn't say I would *do* it." But Adam thought if it got help, it might be worth it.

"Didn't we see some string around here?" Noah asked. "We could let the pail down with that."

Adam hurried to the corner where a package of brushes had been opened. He held up the string. It was pretty strong but only about four feet long. He walked over and sank down on the canvas.

They sat in silence for a while. Finally, Noah went to check up on the woman.

"I didn't cause the blackout," Adam thought. "If we can only get that woman down in time, everything will be all right." He felt as though he'd tried everything. All his good ideas had failed.

Why had he punched that button? Who wanted to see an old roof, anyway?

Noah looked worried when he came back. He flopped down beside Adam. "She says if anyone can get that old chopper, you can."

"She does?" Adam was surprised. Suddenly he jumped up. "I've got it!" he yelled.

"What's your great idea now?" Noah didn't move.

"You're sitting on it! We wanted a flag, didn't we? Well, we have one. Better than that old shirt of yours."

"The canvas? We can't hold it up. It's too big and heavy."

"Sure it's big. They covered the floor with it when they painted the ceiling. But we're not going to hold the sign up."

Noah wasn't sure what they would do with it, but he jumped up to help. He thought that the woman ought to be in the hospital right now.

They pushed the tools and papers aside and laid the canvas flat. They decided on black for the sign because the gray canvas was spotted with white paint. The helicopter might not come very close, but Adam wanted the pilot to notice it right away.

"We'll put 'Channel 4' at the top," he said. "That will be like calling his name."

"Make it big. Make it look like yelling."

Adam printed CHANNEL 4 in four-foot-high letters near the top of the canvas. "Now what?"

" 'Woman having baby on roof any minute'?"

"She is?" Adam looked white.

"Well, by the time they get here maybe she will be," Noah said. He ran outside to see where the helicopter was.

Adam thought that perhaps the pilot didn't want to get mixed up with the woman any more than he did. He printed WOMAN ON ROOF NEEDS HOSPITAL!

"It's still flying in long swoops up and down the city," Noah came back and reported. He saw what Adam had written and added FAST in big letters underneath.

They dragged the heavy canvas out onto the roof. They had to fold it to get it through the door, and the letters blurred a little, but they could still read the message.

"Now we heave it over the wall and hang on to it," Adam said.

"We do? I thought we'd just spread it out here."

"You wanted a flag, didn't you? This building is the tallest one around. The pilot will see it blocks away."

It was a terrible job to get the big canvas up and over the wall. When it was half over they felt it slipping away from them.

"Pull it back," Adam yelled. "We're losing it!"

They tugged hard and hauled it back onto the roof.

Adam fell backward and then put his head in his hands.

For the first time Noah felt sorry for his friend. Adam had caused a lot of trouble but he had tried to get them out of it.

He glanced at the helicopter. On its next trip to the river it might be close enough to see their flag. If only they didn't have to hold it in place.

"Adam!" he cried. "The ladder is heavy. We can let *it* hold the canvas. We can tie it on with the string!"

They ran inside and brought out the ladder. It was certainly heavy. Adam went back for the string and a screwdriver to make holes in the canvas. Noah went over to report their progress to the woman.

By the time Noah got back Adam had made one hole at the end of the canvas. He had made it above the hem, where it was easier to get through the heavy material. He hoped the hem would keep it from tearing.

They made another hole at the other end and one in the middle.

"It's coming," Noah said, looking up. "We'll have to hurry."

The string was hard to cut. The screwdriver wasn't very sharp and they had to chop and chop. But they finally had three pieces.

They tied the canvas to the ladder, which lay against the wall. As they pulled and lifted the canvas, it gradually swung down the side of the building. Adam held his breath. The string held.

"I guess I'd better tell her to get ready." Noah ran back to the woman.

The helicopter began to circle when it was five blocks away.

"Good news!" Noah came back and reported. "When she saw the chopper coming the pains stopped."

"Does that mean she's not —?"

"Oh, no. They just stopped because she's worried. She's a little scared of flying."

"I can't see why she's scared of that. She should be grateful to us."

"She is. She said if the baby's a boy she'll name it after you."

Adam grinned for the first time since he'd punched the button.

The plane stopped its circle and headed down Locust Street, four blocks away from the Dixon Building.

"Quick, let's shake it," Noah cried.

They both bent down and grabbed an end of the ladder. They kept lifting the ladder and dropping it until they saw the chopper turn toward them.

Then they leaned over the wall and waved and hollered. They could hardly hear themselves as the helicopter circled above them.

Noah ran toward the bench and pointed. Adam ran over and pointed to the S.O.S.

The pilot leaned out and made a sweeping gesture.

"He's coming down," Adam yelled. "He wants us out of the way!"

They raced inside the room where the elevator was and looked out a window.

The pilot put the helicopter gently down on the S.O.S.

A man got out of the passenger seat and ducked under the still-whirling blades. The boys ducked too, even though the blades were well above their heads.

"I hope you kids really mean it," the man said.

"We do," Noah replied. He walked with the man toward the bench.

Adam ran around to the other side of the chopper.

"Nice landing," he said to the pilot.

"Yeah. What are you kids doing on the roof?"

Adam hesitated. "We're helping the woman," he said. "What caused the power failure?"

"Air conditioners. Everyone had to have their air conditioners on."

Adam hadn't thought of that. There certainly hadn't been any on the roof.

The man and Noah helped the woman over to the helicopter and the pilot whistled when he saw her. "You weren't kidding," he said.

The woman smiled and waved to Adam.

He waved back. "My name's Adam," he called above the roar of the engine.

"Any room for us?" Noah sounded hopeful. "We're stuck up here."

"No," the pilot said. "I'll just about get her up as it is. Electricity will be on within the hour. Take your sign down. There's a police copter flying around too."

The boys went inside and watched the helicopter rise in the air and whirl away.

After they had dragged the canvas and ladder inside, they sat down to wait. First, Adam put the pail between the elevator doors so they wouldn't close if the electricity went on and someone pushed a button down below.

"If we could have gotten a ride in the copter it would have been worth it," Noah said.

"It was worth it." Adam lay back on the canvas and closed his eyes. "Zappo," he murmured.

4. Ghosts

Adam was a spaceman. As he went up the steps to Noah's front door he didn't feel as happy about his costume as he had when he'd put it on at home. He wondered how Noah would look as a robot.

When he rang the bell it was answered by a ghost.

"Oh, hello," Adam said. "Is Noah home?"

The ghost laughed and flapped its arms under the sheet.

"I fooled you! I guess no one will know me in this thing!"

"Noah, you're not a robot! You said you were going to be a robot."

"Well, that didn't work out. I'm a ghost. What are you?"

"What *am* I?" Adam was indignant. "I'm a spaceman, just as I said I was going to be!"

Noah looked Adam up and down. "Oh, sure. You're a spaceman, all right, I guess."

"You guess? Look, this is really my football helmet but I covered it with silver foil."

"Sure," Noah agreed. "And now it looks — well — sort of like a space helmet. That's kind of a big jacket you've got on. Is it your father's?"

"No, it's my sister's boyfriend's. He's a jogger. I'll put my mask on later because it's still pretty early. We might as well wait here."

The boys sat down on Noah's top step.

"I wish this was Halloween, so we could go around ringing doorbells and getting treats instead of going to that dumb party at the playground," Noah grumbled.

"So do I." Adam pushed his helmet back. "It's nice of them to have a dress-up party at the playground in August, though. We can practice for the real thing. And there's going to be a parade — and prizes for the best costumes." Adam looked down at his pants. He hadn't been able to do much about them.

"I bet there will be a lot of ghosts." Noah loosened the necktie that held his sheet in place. "There always are, because ghosts are easy."

"Girls will probably get all the prizes. They're good at costumes. I wonder what Bootsy and Anne and Mary Ellen will be."

"Bootsy would make a good jockey," Noah said.

"Mary Ellen will be a nurse, I bet, and Anne — well — Anne could be Snow White."

"Say, you *do* like Anne. Snow White!" Noah punched Adam on the shoulder.

"I just said she could be Snow White. That doesn't mean anything." Adam looked grumpy for a while.

Soon a small group came down the street, headed for the playground. A woman in a green dress pushed a stroller in which sat a little boy in a fireman's hat. He was shaking a rattle. Another woman walked beside her, closely followed by a bunch of what looked like animals. At least they had tails.

Noah stood up and flapped and hooted. The animals scampered ahead of the women. Noah felt better about his costume.

Ten kids in the next group were bigger than the animals. There were two ghosts and a spaceman among them.

"Well, we might as well get started." Adam put on a small mask and pulled down his helmet.

Noah tightened the necktie. He stumbled going down the steps because he couldn't see very well. Adam helped him pull down the sheet so he could see out of the eye holes, and they started off.

"I have a dollar to buy stuff," Adam said. "There will be cotton candy and ice cream and things like that."

"I have a dollar too, but I don't see how I can eat with this thing on."

Adam looked at his friend. The sheet didn't have any hole for a mouth. "Well, you can't get much for a dollar anyway," he said.

The boys stopped at the corner nearest the playground entrance. From all four directions came clowns, spacemen, firemen, devils, angels, Red Riding Hoods, robots, Supermen, Batmen, and ghosts.

Two boys wore a horse costume. They trotted and pranced and kicked up their heels. The crowd laughed and clapped.

"There goes first prize," Adam said.

A clown with a painted face waved to them.

"Who's that?" Noah asked. "He knows us."

"Look at that little guy in that awful mask," Noah exclaimed. "Who is he supposed to be?"

"The Incredible Hulk. Say, that does look funny on a little guy," Adam said.

The streetlights flashed on as the boys went into the playground. They walked around first to see what there was to buy. Hot dogs were seventy-five cents; sodas, twenty-five; cotton candy and candied apples were fifty cents apiece.

"I wouldn't get very much to eat here," Noah said. "Not for a dollar, even if I could find my mouth."

Suddenly two floodlights lit up the center of the playground. Music blared from a loud-speaker.

The noise was a signal to the crowd to start running and shouting. Supermen and animals, clowns and cowboys, dashed around in the circle of light. The horse boys trotted and pranced in the center and the crowd yelled and jumped up and down to see better.

Adam stood in the shadow at the edge of the circle and watched.

"Hey, look at those Indians dancing! And those big kids dressed as pirates." He turned to the ghost at his side.

"Noah, look over there!"

The ghost didn't answer. Adam put a hand on its shoulder.

The ghost gave a deep cough, pulled away, and disappeared in the crowd.

Adam felt hurt at Noah's acting that way. Then he realized that it hadn't been Noah at all. The shoulder he'd touched had been too high for Noah's and the cough had been too low.

Adam felt uneasy. It was fun not knowing who the other kids were but it was spooky not knowing your best friend. He started to wander through the crowd looking for ghosts.

"If I know Noah," he thought, "he's going to be looking at food whether he can eat it or not." He headed back into the shadows where the men selling food stood around the edges of the playground.

He felt a tug on his sleeve and looked down.

The Incredible Hulk looked up at him through its rubbery mask.

"Adam, that's you, isn't it?" it said.

"Yes," he said uncertainly.

The figure pushed the mask off its face and up onto the top of its head. It was Bootsy.

"You didn't know me, did you?" she asked.

"Well, maybe not at first," Adam admitted.

"I've lost Anne and Mary Ellen," she said.

"How did you know me?" Adam asked.

"I'm not sure. You just looked like Adam. Where's Noah?"

"I'm looking for him."

"What is he?"

"A ghost."

"Oh. Well, it's not easy to find the right ghost around here."

Just then the music stopped and a voice over the loud-speaker announced that there would be a parade of children under five years old.

"Let's go watch the little kids. They're cute," Bootsy said. "Maybe we'll see the others over there."

On the way back to the circle of light Adam kept an eye out for ghosts. He saw two, but they were the wrong size. Anyway, they didn't pay any attention to him. Noah would certainly recognize him because no one else had thought of making a football helmet into a space helmet.

"Did you see that policeman?" Bootsy asked. "That's a great costume. I wish I'd thought of that."

The parade wouldn't begin for another ten minutes, so Adam and Bootsy decided to buy something to eat.

As they made their way to the venders, Adam saw an angel he thought might be Anne, but Bootsy just passed it by. He saw one ghost, but he thought it might be the one that had fooled him before. He hadn't liked the way it had given that deep cough and disappeared. They passed the lady in the green dress pushing the boy in the stroller. His fireman's hat was off and he was asleep.

"Let's get in the candy apple line," Bootsy said. "It's shorter."

Some girls Bootsy knew got in back of them and Bootsy pulled down her mask to show them.

Two big boys dressed as pirates began to jeer.

"Look at that little Hulk!" one called. "The Incredible must have laid an egg!"

Adam shifted from foot to foot. He smelled trouble.

"I guess I can be whatever I want!" Bootsy yelled back. "You're nothing but stupid old pirates!"

"Do you know what pirates do?" One boy came up close to Bootsy. "They take anything they want! Let me try that mask." His hand shot out and grabbed it.

Bootsy jerked her head and the mask snapped back hard against her face. Her foot shot out and kicked the pirate in the shin.

The pirate let out a surprised "Ooff" and stepped back.

Adam was mad, and disgusted with Bootsy. Why didn't she know not to make things worse when a big guy picked on her? He wanted to fade right into the crowd and disappear.

"Oh, you're tough are you?" the pirate snarled. He began to circle her as the kids scattered. "We'll see how tough the peewee Hulk is!"

Adam knew that the thing to do was leave — fast. He also knew that he had to take Bootsy with him.

He watched the pirate circling Bootsy as she turned slowly to face him. Suddenly Adam let out a terrible yell and, head down, ran straight at the pirate. His helmet whammed into the pirate just below his ribs. Adam staggered but kept his feet under him. As the pirate fell over backward Adam turned, grabbed Bootsy's hand, and ran.

They ran, weaving around animals, men from outer space, bandits, all the masked chattering figures, and ended up at the far corner of the playground. There they stopped, gasping for breath.

"Take off that mask," Adam ordered.

Bootsy pulled it off and crammed it into her

pocket. "You're right. They won't know me now," she said.

Adam took off his helmet and peeled off the silver foil.

"Thanks, Adam," Bootsy said. "That was a neat trick."

"Neat because it worked." Adam put the helmet back on. "If it hadn't, both pirates would have jumped me."

"Then I would have rescued you."

"Sure," he said. He was sure she would have tried, anyway. "I'm ready to leave. I've had enough of this party."

"Me too, but I have to find Mary Ellen and Anne. We have to walk home together."

"I have to find Noah."

They wandered around for a while looking for their friends and keeping an eye out for the pirates.

A clown hailed them. It wore baggy pants, a crazy top, and a high smashed-up hat. Its face was painted with a big smile and its nose was very red.

"Hi, Anne," Bootsy said. "I've been looking for you."

Adam was speechless. For a minute he refused to believe this funny-looking creature was pretty Anne of the shiny, yellow hair. Looking more closely he saw that the hair was pinned up under the hat. It was Anne, all right.

"Where's Mary Ellen?" Bootsy asked.

"Saving my place in the hot dog line," Anne answered, "while I look for you. What are you supposed to be, Adam?"

"Nothing," he muttered.

Just then they heard a strangled shout behind them. "Adam, oh Adam, help!"

Adam's heart sank. Had the pirates tackled Noah? He didn't think that his trick would work a second time.

The three ran toward the repeated shouts. They pushed their way through a knot of people. In the center stood Noah. His sheet was twisted around his head and the woman in the green dress was holding him firmly by the shoulder.

"He stole my wallet!" she was yelling. "Get the police! He stole my wallet!"

In Noah's hand was a bright red wallet.

Adam went over to Noah and pulled the sheet around so that Noah could see out of the eye holes.

"Adam, I didn't steal it," Noah said. "I saw it on the ground, so I picked it up. Then this woman grabbed me and began saying I stole it!"

"Look, lady. Noah doesn't steal things," Adam said.

"Police, police!" the woman shouted. The little guy in the stroller began to cry.

A tall figure broke through the crowd.

"It's a policeman," Bootsy said. "I mean it's a *real* policeman. I thought it was just a costume."

Anne looked at the tall figure in blue. "It's a policewoman," she said.

The officer tried to listen to the woman and Noah, who were both talking at the same time.

"We'll go over to the police station and straighten this out," she said. "There is a special room for kids' problems."

"I'm coming with you," Adam told the policewoman.

"Fine," she said.

"I'm coming too," Bootsy said.

"I'll get Mary Ellen and meet you there." Anne ran off.

"A ghost bumped into me," the woman told the policewoman. "When I saw that my purse was open I turned, and there he was holding my wallet."

Bootsy lagged behind for a minute, then she ran and caught up with Adam.

"I've got an idea," she said. "I'm going back to the playground, but I'll be at the station in a little while."

Bootsy was gone before Adam could stop her. Everything was going wrong. He thought the pirates would really get her this time.

Inside the station was a small room with benches around two sides. There was a large desk with a gray-haired man sitting at it. He didn't have a hat on and his blue jacket was unbuttoned, but he was a real cop, all right.

"What have you got, Officer Coleman? A ghost and a — well — football-jogger?" he asked.

"The ghost and Mrs. —?" the policewoman began.

"Wilson," the woman said.

"— and Mrs. Wilson were involved in an incident at the costume party at the playground, Captain."

"Noah didn't take the wallet," Adam said.

"Let's have the parties not involved in this affair take a seat and wait quietly," the captain suggested.

Officer Coleman pointed to the bench and Adam sat. The woman in the green dress pushed the stroller to the far end of Adam's bench.

"I just *found* the wallet. I didn't take it," Noah told the captain.

"You have to be accused before you can defend yourself, son," the captain said. "And take that sheet off so I can see you. Now, Mrs. Wilson, what happened?"

Mrs. Wilson talked and talked. She told the captain all about how kids were brought up wrong and how they should be brought up. The captain listened.

Noah tried to loosen the necktie that held his sheet, but he had yanked at it so much that he couldn't undo the knot.

As Mrs. Wilson was talking, the door opened and Bootsy, her mask in place, slipped into the room. She went over to Adam and whispered, "I've got a bunch of ghosts outside. When I bring them in, keep that woman looking somewhere else." Then she darted out again.

Adam slid slowly along the bench toward the stroller. He would help, of course, but he was jealous. He liked to be the one with good ideas. He watched the door.

"Yes, I have the wallet back," Mrs. Wilson was saying. "But children shouldn't be allowed to get away with —"

The door opened and Adam's hand reached for the push bar of the stroller. He shook it and the kid whimpered. He shook harder and the kid hollered. Mrs. Wilson turned quickly toward her child.

Bootsy held the door wide and four ghosts walked in. She shoved them over to surround Noah.

"Now," she said to the captain, "let that woman pick out the ghost that bumped into her and took her old wallet!"

"You can't burst in here like that!" Officer Coleman said.

"It's a line-up," Bootsy explained to the captain. "She said a ghost bumped into her. OK, which ghost?"

"Bootsy's smart, all right," Adam thought. "I'm glad I got her away from that pirate."

"This — this Incredible Hulk is a friend of these two boys. I had no idea what she was up to." Officer Coleman was upset.

"She's ahead of us," the captain admitted. "Take off your mask," he said to Bootsy.

Adam saw him smile when he saw the real Bootsy.

"So you rounded up all the ghosts, did you? How did you get them to come here?" he asked.

"I offered them fifty cents apiece."

"Well, as long as they are here, what about it, Mrs. Wilson? Which one did bump into you and take the wallet?" the captain asked.

"How do I know? They all look alike!" Mrs. Wilson snapped. The kid continued to holler. "I grabbed the one who had it!"

"We know the one who picked it up. The question is, who stole it?" He looked at the five ghosts.

"I can't stay here all night," Mrs. Wilson said. "It's way past Sonny's bedtime."

"Why don't you go home, Mrs. Wilson? You have your wallet; we'll settle who took it," the captain suggested.

The woman cop helped Mrs. Wilson out the door with the stroller.

The ghosts, except for Noah, buzzed in an angry group around Bootsy.

"Now, young lady," the captain said to her. "These are all the ghosts who were at the playground?"

Bootsy went over and whispered to him.

"All right," he said. "Officer Coleman will go with you. You'd better take Sergeant Jones along too," he added to the policewoman.

The ghosts trooped after Bootsy.

"Just a minute," he called to them. "You ghosts sit down and wait a while. This may be interesting." He opened a newspaper.

Noah sat down beside Adam and they finally got the necktie untied. Noah looked pretty hot when he pulled the sheet off.

"This is awful," he said. "They won't put me in jail just for picking up a wallet, will they?"

"I don't think so," Adam replied. "I think the captain is on your side. He's on Bootsy's side, anyway."

The door opened a little way and a clown and a figure in a long green gown, a small green hat, and a green gauze mask over its nose and mouth came quietly in.

The captain looked up from his paper. "Trouble?" he asked.

"No," the clown said. "We're just friends of Adam and Noah."

"Trouble enough." The captain went back to his newspaper.

The newcomers sat down beside the boys.

"We were surprised to find that you're a clown," Noah said to Anne. "Adam thought that you'd be —"

Adam kicked Noah's leg. "You must be Mary Ellen." He looked at the figure in green. "We thought you'd be a nurse because you're going to be one."

"I changed my mind." Mary Ellen pulled the mask off. "I'm going to be a doctor."

"Doctors don't go around looking like that," Adam protested.

"When they operate they do," Mary Ellen said. "Maybe I'll operate on you someday, Adam."

"I'm very healthy," Adam said quickly. "What took you so long?" he asked Anne. "You said you'd be right back."

"I lost Mary Ellen. She wasn't in the hot dog line where I left her."

"Two tough pirates pushed me out of line," Mary Ellen explained, "so I joined the apple line and they pushed me out of that too. The police are never around when you want them!"

"Sh, sh," hissed Anne, Noah, and Adam together.

The captain didn't seem to have heard.

"Sometimes they are around when you *don't* want them," Noah whispered to Adam. "If I could have seen straight I'd have thrown that old wallet at that woman and run!"

"Sure," Adam muttered.

Noah looked depressed. The ghosts wiggled and muttered on their bench. The captain began the crossword puzzle.

At last the door opened. Bootsy bounded in looking excited. Next came Officer Coleman and a young policeman with a ghost between them.

The ghost was certainly taller than Noah but not by very much.

"Ah," the captain said. "The last ghost?"

"We were lucky," Officer Coleman said. "He was just leaving."

"Off with that sheet," the captain ordered.

The new ghost fumbled with his costume.

"He's the one I told you about," Bootsy said. "I knew him because of his big feet. He's the only one who wouldn't come along when I offered him fifty cents."

The ghost gave a deep cough.

"Of course," Adam thought. "He's the one I thought was Noah."

"Off with that sheet," the captain barked again.

Sergeant Jones grabbed the cloth and yanked.

A short bald man appeared from under the sheet. He had a silly grin on his face.

"Just a Halloween trick, Your Honor," he said in a deep voice. "No harm done."

"Why, if it isn't Slippery Sam!" the captain said. "When that little girl told me about a ghost with a deep cough, who didn't want to come to the police station even for fifty cents, I thought maybe you were around."

"Just for a little fun, Your Honor. You know how it is."

"You're not talking to a judge yet, Sam. Just call me Captain."

"Sure, Captain, sure. I just joined the kiddies out there for a lark, you know?"

"I know. Search him," the captain ordered Sergeant Jones.

Sergeant Jones pulled a black wallet and a green one out of Sam's jacket pocket. In an inside pocket he found another wallet, a lady's wristwatch, and a string of beads. He tossed them onto the captain's desk.

"Just having fun with the kids, were you?" the captain asked.

"Well, times are hard, Your Honor, Captain, sir." Sam shook his head sadly.

"Yes, especially for people who have their pockets picked," the captain said. "I'm surprised that even you would rob kids."

"Kids? Never!" said Sam. "I never picked a kid's pocket."

"Why the playground, then?"

"Well, Captain, sir, I was working the street leading to the playground and a man got a little mad at me when I bumped him, so I ducked in to the party."

"Do a little work while you were in there, Sam?"

"I told you I don't rob kids. I like kids."

"Come over here, Noah," the captain said.

When Noah was in front of the desk the captain went on.

"Sam, Noah says that he found a wallet on the ground and a woman grabbed him and said he'd stolen it. What color do you think it was?"

"Couldn't say, Your Honor, sir."

"You won't be in any more trouble for trying to get one more wallet than you are now, Sam," the captain said.

Slippery Sam was silent for some time. Finally he sighed and said, "Red."

"Thank you, Sam," the captain said. "OK, Sergeant. Take him across the hall and book him. Have someone trace the owners of these wallets."

"Your Honor, sir, I'd like to thank Slippery Sam," Noah said.

Sam grinned at him and winked at the captain.

When the sergeant had marched Sam out, the captain spoke to Noah.

"OK, son. You can go now," he said. "We'll get in touch with Mrs. Wilson and explain everything to her."

"Thank you, Captain, sir," Noah said.

"While you're thanking everyone, don't forget that little girl." He nodded at Bootsy. "In a few years I hope you'll consider police work," he said to her.

"I have already," Bootsy said, smiling at Officer Coleman.

The four ghosts clustered around Bootsy.

"You owe us fifty cents each," one said. "We want it now."

Bootsy looked at Noah. "They helped a lot," she said. "You didn't go to jail, did you?"

"Well, no," Noah said slowly, "but *I* didn't promise to pay them."

"Come on, Noah." Adam pulled a dollar out of his pocket. "Pay up. It's been kind of interesting, but it's time to go home."

Noah pulled out his dollar too.

The ghosts took the two dollars and scurried out.

"Officer Coleman, you better get back there and keep an eye on those pirates," the captain said. "They sound pretty active."

"Thanks, Bootsy, for finding Slippery Sam," Noah said.

"Noah, *I* saved Bootsy from the pirates," Adam put in. "I bet that's why she helped you."

"I'm through thanking people for tonight." Noah slung the sheet over his arm as they went out.

5. The Chase

Adam ran up the three steps to Noah's front door and punched the bell.

The door opened at once and Noah joined him.

"You said you had a plan for us when you called," Adam said. "It better be good; I ran all the way over."

"Sure it is." Noah reached into his back pocket and held up a five-dollar bill.

"That's good, all right," Adam agreed. "Where did you get it?"

"My mother. It's for us."

"It is? She just gave it to you? Why?"

"Well, there's a rummage sale at the church —" Noah began.

"They're no good," Adam said. "Just a lot of old clothes that are too small."

"Mother was supposed to help sell stuff there but she's tired of rummage sales so she asked if she could send us instead. They need strong boys to move boxes around."

"And we get the five dollars if we help in this dumb rummage sale?" Adam asked. "I knew there was a catch to it!"

"If you're so weak you can't move a few boxes, I'll do it alone and keep the five dollars for myself!" Noah said.

"Weak! Who said I was weak? I bet I could throw you down and take the fiver right out of your pocket!"

"You won't." Noah was sure of that. He kept walking along in the direction of the church while Adam lagged behind.

"How long do we have to stay?" Adam asked finally.

"Mrs. Rodgers will tell us. She's running the whole show."

"Maybe it will be just for a little while." Adam caught up with his friend. "I might buy a good Frisbee with my two fifty. I saw one in the hardware store window. What will you buy?"

Noah didn't answer. They had come to the corner where the church was.

"It looks closed up," Adam said. "Maybe the rummage sale was last week."

"Around back," Noah said. "There's a room in the back of the church that they use for sales."

Noah headed down the side street but he walked very slowly.

"You never know what you'll find at a rummage sale," he said. "That's the fun of it. Sometimes people find an old hunk of jewelry that turns out to be real gold."

"That's the kind of thing that happens to other people," Adam said. "Not us. I'm going to get that Frisbee."

"Maybe we'll find something in here for five dollars that we could both use," Noah suggested.

"No you don't! I want my two fifty!"

"OK, OK. We'll get change for it as soon as we get in."

There were three cars parked in back of the church. The curb was lined with boxes.

Noah took a deep breath. "Adam," he said. "We have to spend the money at the rummage sale."

"What do you mean, we have to? You said that money was ours!"

"It's ours to spend at the sale. My mother said that if she helped she'd have to buy something here. The women who help always buy stuff. So I said we'd come and spend the money."

"Why didn't you tell me?" Adam demanded. "You made me walk all this way and then —"

"It's only four blocks."

A woman beside the cars waved to Noah and called, "Yoo hoo!"

"Noah, that was a dirty trick! I was going to get that Frisbee and now —"

97

Noah trotted toward the woman.

Adam stood still for a moment and then trotted after him.

The woman said that her name was Mrs. Rodgers, and she was so glad to see Adam that he was afraid she would kiss him. Noah was already piled high with boxes and soon disappeared through the back door of the church.

Mrs. Rodgers peeked into the boxes on the curb and quickly made a large red seven on one and fives on two others.

"The tables are numbered," she said. "The women are waiting to price these last things. I'm so glad you want to help!"

Adam carried the boxes into a big room full of long tables. Already the tables were piled high. A woman at table seven opened a box and exclaimed, "How wonderful!"

"Evening dresses!" Adam muttered to Noah as he headed back toward the door. "A whole box of evening dresses!"

More cars drew up to unload. Pretty soon the boys worked out a system. Adam unloaded the cars, Mrs. Rodgers quickly checked and numbered the boxes, and Adam carried them to the door and handed them to Noah, who raced to the right tables.

"You two boys are the best help we've ever had." Mrs. Rodgers was all smiles.

Adam didn't really mind working, but he didn't think he could find something he wanted at the sale. Evening dresses, chipped dishes, baby clothes, picture frames, and muffin tins didn't interest him.

"That does it," Mrs. Rodgers said finally. "We open in ten minutes." She smiled at the people waiting to come in. "Lovely things for sale in there, aren't there, Adam?"

"There are a lot of boxes," Adam said, stretching his arms as he walked inside.

"There's a toy table." Noah came over to him.

"Kid stuff. Broken, too, I bet. You'd better give me my money before you buy a lot of junk."

Mrs. Rodgers dug into her purse and made change for the five-dollar bill. "You boys are so good, to help and also buy!"

Adam thought so too. "Bet there isn't an ounce of gold in the place," he muttered to Noah.

Mrs. Rodgers blew a whistle that hung around her neck and the buzz of women's voices stopped.

"Open in five minutes," she called. "Coffee in the side room, but get someone to take your place if you leave the table. Hold prices as usual."

The boys piled up the now empty boxes in a corner of the room by the door. Mrs. Rodgers said something about taking them out to the curb for the trash man after the sale, but Adam decided he would be gone long before that.

When Mrs. Rodgers opened the door there was a rush of people. Adam thought he had better make sure there wasn't any gold, and he finally found a box of jewelry.

Noah looked at the toy counter. Adam was right, there were a lot of trucks with three wheels. He had some at home like that. He found a few nice little cars, the kind he liked best, for ten cents apiece. The paint was scratched but he could fix that, so he bought five of them and went to find Adam to show him.

Adam was holding a bracelet with blue stones in it.

"For Anne?" Noah exclaimed. "You're going to buy that for a girl?"

Adam dropped the bracelet into the box. "It's not gold and it costs too much."

Adam went by a row of shoes on the floor and he saw something he wanted very much — jogging shoes. Blue and white and almost new!

The chairs for people to sit in while they tried on shoes were full, and Adam didn't dare wait. It was hard to believe that someone hadn't bought them already. He sat on the floor and took off his shoes. He was almost afraid to try on the joggers. What if they didn't fit?

They did, though, with plenty of room for thick socks this year and longer toes next. A dollar fifty wasn't bad for great jogging shoes, but that only left him a dollar.

On the wall near the shoes hung coats — mostly old raincoats. One hook held a briefcase. It was rather worn around the edges but he could tell it was a good leather one. He had often seen men hurrying around the city carrying cases just like it. He wanted it as much as he wanted the shoes, but the price tag read two dollars.

When he found Noah, he didn't recognize him at first because Noah was wearing a red baseball cap.

"Wow, those are some jogging shoes," Noah said. "I bet you can wear them for three or four years. Hey, Mrs. Rodgers brought sandwiches for us. We can eat in the side room, where the coffee is."

As they walked toward the side room Adam stopped.

"Look, a real football shirt."

The shirt was yellow and black and when they opened it up it looked quite clean and had no holes. The ticket read $1.50. Noah held it in front of him.

"It comes down to your knees."

"I have one fifty," Noah said, but he folded the shirt and put it half under a brown sweater.

The sandwiches were large and good and the boys took their time eating them.

"You have a lot of stuff for only a dollar." Adam swallowed the last bite. He thought about leaving right away. It would be nice to walk out with a dollar in his pocket. He hadn't exactly agreed to

stay to the end and put out the boxes. Anyway, Noah had tricked him about spending the money at this old rummage sale. He decided on one more tour of the tables before he left.

Noah went to check on the football shirt. The sweater was gone but the shirt was still there. He bought it at once. He guessed he'd grow before too long.

Adam looked at what was left on the toy table. Not much. He'd about decided on a bag of marbles for one dollar when the woman behind the table said, "If you wait a few minutes, sonny, they will be marked down to half price. You can buy two bags for a dollar."

"I don't want two," Adam said. "What else will be marked half price?"

"Everything in the room," she said. "We always do that at the end to get rid of everything."

Adam raced toward the hooks on the wall. As he arrived, Mrs. Rodgers blew her whistle.

"Everything marked down to half price," she called. "Help us clear the place!"

Adam reached up and grabbed the briefcase. He paid the lady a dollar and shuddered at how close he'd come to buying those marbles.

Half an hour later, when Mrs. Rodgers blew her whistle again to say that the sale was over, Adam was walking by the shoes. There were only a few left and some didn't have any mates.

"Noah!" he yelled. "Help!"

Noah ran over with the football shirt tied around his neck.

"My shoes are gone!" Adam cried.

Noah looked at Adam's feet.

"Not my joggers — my shoes. They've been sold!"

"Did you leave them here? You shouldn't have done that."

"You never forget anything, do you? Someone bought my shoes!"

"Well, those are better than your old shoes. They were kind of scuffed up, weren't they? It's not as if they were new."

"I'm getting out of here. Someone just stole my shoes. Come on. Mrs. Rodgers can move those boxes herself!"

The boys joined the last of the customers going out the back door of the church.

Mrs. Rodgers stood beside the door.

"You lovely boys," she cried. "We couldn't have managed without you." She looked carefully at Adam's face. "Now, we want to give you each a dollar fifty after you have put the trash out by the curb."

Adam hesitated, but only for a moment. He quickly piled his and Noah's loot behind the open door and the boys tackled the boxes. All the other ladies left, but not Mrs. Rodgers. She wanted the trash all neatly piled, and with the three dollars in mind they did a good job.

At last they picked up their stuff from behind the door, and Mrs. Rodgers locked up. She gave them the money and managed to kiss Noah before she hurried away. Adam was too fast for her.

"Wow," Adam said. "That was close. Let's put our stuff in my briefcase and we can take turns carrying it." When he opened the briefcase he noticed a bunch of papers, which he put in one of the empty boxes so they wouldn't blow around. He handed the briefcase to Noah.

When they were halfway to the corner, Noah slowed up. "There was a teddy bear out in the trash. I should have taken it for Bobby."

"I'll just walk very slowly to get used to these shoes," Adam said. "You run back."

Noah handed the briefcase to Adam and took off. He found the bear at once and headed back.

When he got to the front of the church he heard a loud noise. A man stood there banging on the door with both fists. He was yelling, "Open up! Help! Open up!"

Noah stopped for a minute. The man's dark hair was rather long and flopped around as he shook his head. His face was red with anger.

He began to swear. Noah could hardly believe that anyone would swear in front of a church. He hurried on toward Adam.

"There's a crazy man at the church door!" he said, as he stuffed the bear into the briefcase. "He's pounding on it and swearing!"

"Swearing? He's taking chances, all right, swearing at a church!"

"He was yelling 'Open up' and 'Help.' "

"Maybe he isn't crazy," Adam said. "Criminals try to get into a church so the cops can't arrest them. I saw a movie once where a criminal got into a church and the police couldn't get him."

"Stop! Thief!" The man was running toward them.

They ran. In the middle of the block Adam looked over his shoulder. The man was gaining on them. Adam couldn't hear what he was yelling, but he looked like a crazy man, and a fast one, at that.

At the next cross street a bus was letting on passengers. The boys squeezed aboard just before it pulled away.

As they sank down into an empty seat, the face of the man flashed by and he shook his fist at them.

"Good old bus," Noah sighed. "Just in time."

"He yelled 'thief' at us," Adam said. "Maybe he thinks I stole this briefcase. It is a nice one, but I paid good money for it."

"He's a wild man, all right," Noah said. "I bet he is a criminal. No good guy would swear at a church! We were lucky to get away from him even if this bus is going the wrong way."

"Hey," Adam said finally, "we'd better get out. We're a long way from home."

They got out at Harvey's Department Store. There was a fountain in front of the store and the boys sat on its rim.

"We might as well go in and look around as long as we're here," Noah suggested.

"What's the use?" Adam asked. "We'll have to spend another dollar to get home. That leaves us with only fifty cents apiece."

A bus pulled up to the curb in front of them. For a second they stared, as the face of the wild man appeared in a window. When he jumped up to get out of the bus, they raced toward Harvey's and whirled through the revolving door. They headed straight back as far as they could go.

"Wow," Noah said when they stopped. *"That* was a surprise."

"He must have caught the next bus," Adam said.

"Can I help you boys?" A tall, pretty woman smiled at them.

Adam looked around him. "We're in little girl dresses! Let's get out of here."

They made their way through china and women's coats, keeping a careful lookout for the wild man.

They were near the escalator when Noah caught

sight of the man. "There he is," he said. "Let's go up!"

"OK, but wait till there are other people on the escalator. We'll bend down so he can't see us as we get up high."

Bent double they arrived at the second floor.

"Look, the sign says toys are on the third floor. Let's go!" Noah cried.

On the third floor they stood peeking down the escalator for several minutes, but the man didn't show.

They stopped in front of the electric trains, which were whizzing under tunnels, crossing bridges, blowing smoke, and whistling.

"It's nice to shop with no money," Noah said. "You don't have to decide anything."

A bell rang. "Closing time," a salesman said. "Everyone must be out of the store in ten minutes."

The boys moved toward the empty escalators.

"Maybe he went outside when he heard the bell," Noah said.

When they were a third of the way down to the second floor, the wild man stepped onto the up escalator. As soon as he saw them, he started walking backward fast.

Adam, who was in front of Noah, said, "Go back up, quick!"

It wasn't easy to go up the down stairs, but the

man's shouts made them try very hard. They hit the third floor just in time for Noah, who was now leading, to dive under the green cloth that hung from the train table. Adam piled in on top of him.

"Sorry, sir, closing time," they heard the salesman say.

"Two boys came up here. I must get hold of them!"

"Two boys? Yes, I saw them go down just a moment ago."

Noah crawled to the far end of the table. It was harder for Adam with the briefcase, but he squirmed along after him. Noah pushed through the cloth at the end of the table and crawled behind a counter. Adam followed. They could hear the men arguing as they made their way to the far wall.

When they finally dared to sit up, they could see a door marked STAIRS.

Adam peered through a display of baby dolls and saw their man looking under the train table. The salesman was getting angry.

The boys chose their time and crept to the door and through it. They raced down two long flights of stairs and tried the door on the landing. It was locked.

"If he should come down the stairs we'd be trapped here," Adam said, gasping for breath.

Noah was already heading back to the second

floor. That door gave when they pushed it and they found themselves in the furniture department. Adam looked longingly at a couch, but he didn't sit down. He had decided the new shoes must be better for jogging than running. They headed toward the escalators in the middle of the store. They were empty.

"I bet he's still looking for us up in toys," Noah said.

"Or waiting for us down below."

They stood undecided.

A large salesman came up behind them. "Hurry up, boys. Closing time. You don't want to get locked in, do you?"

"No," said Noah. "Oh, no we don't!"

"Go along then," the salesman said.

"After you, sir." Adam made a little bow.

"Nice to see a polite kid." The big man stepped on the moving stairs and the boys got on just in back of him.

As they glided down, Adam felt pleased that he had been nice to the big man in front of him. He decided they'd just stick to him and get safely out of the store.

Just then he felt a tug at his briefcase arm, and the face of their man loomed over him from the up escalator. He let out a little cry, and the salesman in front of him turned sharply. Adam swung his arm around and pushed the grabbing arm away.

"He's stolen something!" the wild man cried, trying to walk down as he went up.

As the three came to the first floor the big salesman turned angrily. He looked at the briefcase.

"Shoplifters?" he said, reaching out a large hand.

But Noah and Adam were racing toward the revolving door and whirled through it.

To their right was the entrance to the subway. Noah gave a dollar to the woman in the ticket window and they ran onto the platform. A lot of people were waiting for trains, and they made their way to the far end of the crowd.

"He's not going to give up chasing us," Noah said.

"No, but at least we can sit down on the train. I'd rather be chased sitting down." Adam glanced at his feet.

"We know he wants your briefcase. I don't see why; it's pretty beat up. I wish you'd never seen it."

"Well, that teddy bear you got only has one ear. If you hadn't gone back for it, the wild man wouldn't be chasing us."

They watched for the wild man at each stop, but he didn't board their car. At the end of the line everyone else got out.

"We'd better stay on and ride back to Harvey's," Adam said. "Then we can get a bus home. If we get out here we'll use all our money paying to get on another train and have to walk home. I don't think I could do that."

Noah didn't say anything. He thought about Adam's buying shoes that didn't fit and the briefcase that had gotten them into all this trouble. He was pleased with the baseball cap, the football jersey, and the little cars he'd bought. Maybe the wild man would have noticed them even if he hadn't gone back for the bear.

The conductor stuck his head in the door. "Miss your stop?" He looked at the two sad figures. "OK, stay aboard."

Finally the train began its journey back.

"What if he's waiting for us at Harvey's?" Noah asked.

"I was thinking maybe if we looked different he wouldn't know us. You could put your baseball cap on and pull it over your face. I could wear the football shirt. He might not know us then."

"You could just leave the old briefcase on the train and he wouldn't *want* to know us."

"It's my briefcase! I paid a dollar for it!"

Noah put on the cap, and the football shirt was plenty big for Adam.

"That briefcase has cost us more than a dollar," Noah said. "*You* paid a dollar, but by the time we get home we'll have spent the three dollars Mrs. Rodgers gave us. Half of that was mine, too. So you paid two fifty and I paid one fifty. For an old briefcase!"

Adam didn't say anything for two stops.

"You're right," he said finally. "I've been thinking. If we see him again and he starts after us I'll tell him I'll sell it to him for a dollar fifty and give you back your money."

"What if he just grabs it?"

"I'll let him have it." Adam sighed.

"Good. I'd better get my stuff out." Noah put the little cars into his pocket, but he had to hold the bear. Adam didn't like to be seen with Noah holding it, but he kept quiet.

They got off at Harvey's Department Store and started up the stairs to the sidewalk. When they were near the top Noah went first, to peek through the railing.

"He's there, all right — leaning against a streetlight," he reported.

Adam started to back down the stairs.

"You promised," Noah cried, "and there's a police car at the curb. I'll tell the cop about the wild man's swearing at a church if he causes any trouble."

Adam still seemed uncertain.

"Maybe you can sell it for five dollars."

Adam straightened the football shirt, went up the steps, and walked toward the figure leaning against the pole.

The wild man didn't look wild anymore. He seemed limp and tired, but he suddenly stiffened as he realized that it was Adam inside the yellow football shirt. Noah pushed back his cap and moved to the curb.

"I'll sell you this briefcase," Adam said shakily.

The man reached out and took it. He opened it quickly and looked inside. Letting out a groan, he sank to the curb.

A car door opened beside Noah and a policeman looked down at the man. A few passers-by stopped to watch. The policeman glanced at Adam.

"Did you tackle him?" he asked.

Adam shook his head.

Noah went over beside Adam to explain, but he wasn't sure how to begin.

"Move on!" the policeman said to the crowd. "Can you stand up?" he asked the man.

"It's empty," the man said, ignoring him. "A whole year's work. And my wife —"

"Sure," the policeman said. "I understand."

"No, you don't," the man yelled, angry again. "I had all my research papers in this old briefcase ready to be typed, and she sent it to a rummage sale! And then those kids ran away with it!"

"I bought it!" Adam said. "We worked hard at that rummage sale and I spent good money for it!"

"I've followed you all over town and you just ran away!"

"He pounded on the church door and swore!" Noah cried.

"Quiet," the policeman said in a harsh voice. "What did you do with the papers that were in the briefcase?" He looked at the boys.

"Put them in the trash." Adam edged away a little.

The wild man put his hands over his face.

"Mrs. Rodgers said we had to be neat with the trash," Noah said. "Adam put them in one of the empty boxes so they wouldn't blow away."

The wild man grabbed Adam's arm and called, "Taxi, taxi!"

"Hold it," the policeman said. "My buddy will drive you to the church."

He settled the man in the front seat of the police car and the boys in back and explained the situation to the cop behind the wheel. "Stay with them while they look for the papers, and then see the kids home safe."

Adam had remembered to pick up the briefcase. It was nice to have it even if it had caused a lot of trouble.

"It's great to get a ride home," Noah said, "and it saves us fifty cents apiece."

"I still owe you a dollar," Adam said loudly. "We had to take a bus ride and a subway ride when we didn't want to."

"Don't worry about a dollar if you find those papers," the wild man said over his shoulder.

"I had to spend a dollar too," Adam said.

"Five, for the papers. Can't you go faster?" the man asked the driver. "No one will arrest you."

"Nice and easy," the cop said. "We're going to take it nice and easy no matter what happens."

Adam began to worry about finding the papers. There had been a lot of boxes.

It looked like a mountain of trash when they drew up behind the church. The wild man leaped out of the car and began to open boxes and throw them aside.

"Stop." The policeman put a heavy hand on his shoulder. "Think, son. What were you doing when you found the papers? Where were you?" He looked at Adam.

It seemed like a long time ago but Adam closed his eyes and thought.

"We had piled up all the stuff," he said slowly. "Mrs. Rodgers got out a key to lock the door. I ran in and got my things from just inside." He went over to the door and walked slowly back toward the curb. "I opened the briefcase to put them in it." He slowly opened it. "I took out the papers and walked over to the top box on this end and put them in — this one."

"Go on," Noah urged. "Open it!"

Slowly, with three pairs of eyes watching closely, Adam opened the box. The papers were there.

The wild man hugged Adam and said he didn't know how to thank him.

"Five dollars will do it," the cop said.

Noah climbed into the police car. "We've traveled a lot today, but at least we got what we wanted at the sale."

"I'm not sure it was worth it. This briefcase is pretty beat up," Adam said.

Noah didn't say anything.

6. The Island

The boys had checked the weather report. Adam had studied the map in the newspaper and called the Weather Bureau twice. Noah had listened to the radio.

They stood beside Dan on the Nelson Company wharf while the old sailor examined the sky.

"Those fellows don't know everything," Dan said.

"The map showed high pressure all around us," Adam said. "Those little rain lines were a thousand miles away!"

Dan pushed his white sailor hat back a little and spat into the river.

"Sailors don't trust the weather, ever."

"We want to go upriver this time," Adam said. "Up as far as we can until the tide changes, and then come home with it."

The three looked at the blue sky — free of even

the smallest cloud. The river was calm and almost empty of boats at seven o'clock in the morning.

Dan looked downriver at the bridge that had caused the boys so much excitement on their last trip.

"No bridges upstream," he remarked. "And the weather might hold, at that."

The boys put on their life jackets and climbed into the Ark.

"Forget your grub?" Dan asked.

"We've got money instead," Noah answered. "We're going ashore to get hamburgers. There are lots of places up there where the highway runs along the river."

"What if someone steals that craft of yours?" Dan asked.

"We'd never leave the Ark alone," Adam said firmly. "Not after we met Bogey!"

"And if you get in trouble on the river?" Dan untied the painter.

"Head for shore and walk back!" the boys chorused.

"Which shore?" Dan still held the rope.

"This shore!" they cried together.

Dan nodded, tossed the rope aboard, and with a large foot shoved the Ark away from the wharf.

The boys sat side by side on the middle seat, each gripping an oar with both hands. They rowed briskly toward the middle of the river, then, with a wave to Dan, they swung upstream and began to stroke easily and slowly.

In the cool morning air it was fun to row. The tide helped them along and soon they rounded the first bend and came to the River Sailing Club. They stopped rowing for a moment and drifted along.

Then they bent to their oars again, and the next hour seemed very long. It began to get warmer and the air had lost its sparkle. They rested on their oars a lot.

Noah sighed and squirmed around to look upriver. "It's hotter, but the sun isn't so bright."

"It's getting a little hazy," Adam agreed, "and kind of muggy. That's what makes it harder to row."

"Maybe around the next bend there will be a place to eat," Noah said. "Can we make it that far?"

"Sure we can," Adam said. "Let's just row slow and steady and not stop to rest. Stroke — str-o-ke!"

Neither boy wanted to be the first one to stop and rest, so they kept going for a long time. At last, dripping wet from their effort, they came to the bend. Just before they rounded it Adam peered downriver. There was so much mist that he couldn't make out the sailing club dock.

"It looks awfully funny back there," he said uneasily.

"Kind of foggy," Noah agreed. "I'm glad we're not there now."

A few strong strokes took them around the bend. The river widened gradually all the way from the bridge and it lay broad and sunny before them.

"There's the highway," exclaimed Noah. "I bet we'll find a hamburger stand soon." He pulled hard on his oar and the Ark swung around in a circle. "Row, Adam," he yelled. "We're almost there!"

"Look at that," Adam exclaimed. "Just look over there!" He pointed to the middle of the river. "A real island. I didn't know there were islands in the river."

"Maybe after lunch we can row around it," Noah suggested.

"Let's get a little closer now," Adam urged. "If we like it, we can bring our grub out here and have a picnic on the island."

"First why don't we —" Noah began.

"Let's see if we can land first," Adam said. "No use taking our grub out there if we can't land, is there? We'd eat sooner if we knew we weren't going to picnic there."

Noah felt a little confused but didn't argue. "That island is pretty big," he said as they drew nearer. "It must be about as big as a football field."

"It's hard to tell how wide it is from the side," Adam said. "Let's go out a little farther and around the end so we can see both sides."

When they were about twenty yards off the end of the island they rested on their oars.

"Say, it's wide," Adam said. "Maybe as big as two football fields."

"Look at the rocks," Noah said. "We'd have to be careful not to bang the Ark on them."

A strong puff of cold wind suddenly shot the Ark forward.

The boys looked around and saw what looked like a gray curtain at the bend of the river. Another, stronger puff swung the Ark all the way around.

"That's a storm!" Noah cried. "We'd better head for shore!"

"We can't make shore!" Adam yelled. "Pull for the island!"

"Dan said *our* shore." But Noah grabbed his oar and pulled too.

"I — we're the captains of this ship," Adam said. "Captains are bosses in a storm."

The wind blew them hard toward the rocks at the end of the island. It was all they could do — four hands on one oar — to pull the Ark around the point. Sharp, hard rain fell as they struggled.

The bank on one side of the island looked a little less dangerous, but rocks stuck out of the shallow

water. Adam eased over the side of the boat and tugged on the painter. Finally Noah climbed out too, and slipping on the slimy underwater rocks they managed to get the Ark to shore. They pushed it as far as they could under some over-hanging bushes and tied the painter with two half hitches around a tree stump.

They crawled up the low bank and fell down, tired out, under a swaying hemlock tree.

"Wow! That was fast." Noah shivered in his wet clothes. "One minute all calm and sunny, then whoosh, bang!"

"Summer storms are like that," Adam said. "They go fast, too. I bet this blows right on up the river."

"Dan was right." Noah's teeth were chattering. "Those weathermen don't know everything."

They sat huddled under the dripping tree, watching the rain dance on the river. The storm had lost most of its violence and the rain became steady.

"My life jacket is all wet and cold," Noah com-plained. "I wish we hadn't promised — hey! We're on land now! We can take them off."

The boys jumped up and worked on the knots that tied the orange jackets. The ties had shrunk because they were wet, and their struggles in the water had pulled them tight. Finally they were off.

"That's better." Adam sat down again. "It's fun to be alone on an island."

"I guess we're alone." Noah rubbed his arms to warm them.

"Who else would be here?" Adam asked.

"How should I know? Maybe some other ship-wrecked sailors."

"We're not really sailors and we're not ship-wrecked," Adam said. "You're always imagining things."

"I'm not —" Noah stopped. There was a rustling sound in the leaves in back of them.

"That's just a squirrel, I guess." Adam didn't sound too sure.

"How would a squirrel get out here?" Noah whispered. "They don't swim, do they?"

"It could have come out by boat," Adam whispered back.

"Why are you whispering if it's only a squirrel?"

"Because you are," Adam said impatiently. "Look, here we are on our first island and you're scared!"

"I'm not scared. I just wish we'd gone ashore first and gotten our —"

"Don't," said Adam.

They were silent for quite a while. The rain came down heavily. The wet branches overhead creaked and swayed.

"Our teacher said that Indians lived along this

river a long time ago. I bet they knew this island," Adam said. "Let's explore."

"Maybe, when it stops raining," Noah agreed.

"You'll want to go for food then. I don't think we can get any wetter than we are now. Let's start!" Adam got up.

"I'll stay and watch the Ark." Noah didn't move.

"No you don't!" Adam exclaimed. "If I explore, you do too! You're just scared!"

"I am not," Noah insisted. "I just feel weak because I'm so hun — you know."

"Forget it," Adam said. "If you do something, you'll forget your stomach. Come on and prove you're not scared."

Noah got up fast. "If you say I'm scared again I'll —"

"OK, OK," Adam put in quickly. "You go along that shore and I'll take this one. Then we'll come back and report."

Noah hesitated. "We ought to have a signal. I think scouts have signals."

"Good idea," Adam agreed. "If either of us finds something interesting, come back here and give a wolf call."

"OK, scout." Noah headed around the point on the side of the island that faced the highway.

Adam started down the other side. He tried to walk along the little bank but the underbrush was very heavy. Prickly bushes grew along the edge and hung over the water. He retreated and made his way among the trees.

He began to feel very alone. He couldn't hear Noah at all. He felt a little ashamed of having teased him about being afraid. Having done so, he was determined to prove that he wasn't afraid himself. He couldn't be the first back at the hemlock, so he pressed on. He slid on wet leaves twice and fell down. He paused several times to listen for a wolf call.

Climbing over a fallen tree trunk, he saw a tiny cove nestled in a break in the underbrush. A canoe was drawn up on the low bank.

He stopped short and the hair on the back of his head stirred a little. It wasn't a birch bark canoe — it wasn't even a wooden one; it was made of aluminum.

"We're not alone," he whispered.

"Ow-oo-oo," came faintly through the woods.

Adam turned, scrambled over the tree trunk, and fought his way back to the hemlock as fast as he could.

Noah was there, looking white and shaken. "I saw them," he gasped. "In the middle. I heard them — oh, Adam!"

"Who?" Adam demanded. "I saw a canoe on shore. Sit down and tell me!"

Noah sank down under the tree. "Two men — they're murderers!"

Adam whistled softly and looked at Noah. There was no doubt that he was very upset.

"Did they see you?" he asked.

Noah shook his head.

"Just tell me what you heard," Adam said. "What did they say?"

"It's hard to remember," Noah said in a shaky voice. "One said, 'We'll have to get rid of Fred first.' The other said something about maybe there should be a car accident."

"What else did they say?" Adam urged.

"Well, the one called Tony said that they would have to decide about the other two today. He said getting rid of them would be harder."

"Decide what?" Adam asked.

Noah thought. "I don't know," he said finally. "Let's go, Adam. I don't mind rowing in the rain."

"Let me think a minute and you just rest."

Adam remembered how frightened, or maybe surprised, he'd been when he saw the canoe. Also how spooky it had been all alone in the wet woods. He thought maybe Noah had scared himself.

"It's hard to tell from what they said," he began. "Maybe Fred is a dog that they can't keep anymore. Maybe they live in a small apartment and Fred's a big dog."

"What about the other two?"

"Well, maybe Fred had puppies and they —"

"Dogs named Fred don't have puppies," Noah

insisted. "They didn't say anything about an apartment. We ought to go and find the Coast Guard captain right away." He got up and grabbed his life jacket.

"The captain won't like it if we say these guys are murderers and they're not," Adam objected. "We can't prove they are."

"I don't think we want to prove it."

"What did they look like?"

"Tony was older than the other one. He was mad that the other one — the one with the beard — laughed a lot."

"I don't think murderers laugh," Adam said.

"You know all about murderers, don't you? You didn't even see them!"

"You're sure they didn't see you?" Adam asked.

Noah was sure.

"OK, let's creep up on them like scouts. If they say anything to prove that they are murderers we can take off right away. Say! We could push their canoe into the river and they would be stuck on the island until the Coast Guard comes!"

"Serve them right." Noah stood holding his life jacket. "But I don't want —"

"You could be the scout leader and find your trail back to them," Adam went on. "We'll just get near enough to prove that you're right."

Noah hesitated.

"Lead on, scout. I'll follow," Adam said quickly.

Noah dropped the jacket and grinned. He led the way around the side of the island that faced the highway, stepping high and carefully. He avoided twigs that might snap and held branches aside until Adam could put up a hand to catch them.

Soon they came to a little clearing where the underbrush gave way to a carpet of pine needles. Noah stopped and listened. Adam shivered a little when he heard the rumble of men's voices.

Noah dropped to his knees and crawled across the open space and over to a little ridge of earth covered with high ferns. Adam followed him silently. They crouched low and listened. One man was laughing.

"Stop kidding around," the other cut in. "This is serious. We've got to get this planned fast. There's a time limit, you know."

Adam put up his hand and gently parted a clump of ferns. Through the little hole he could see a very small clearing. On the far side of it two men sat under a pine tree. The bearded one lay sprawled, his long denim-covered legs stretched out. The other one, a red-visored cap on the back of his head, sat cross-legged beside him.

The man in the cap went on. "Come on, Jack. You said that you could think on the island. No one around, no telephone, no doorbell or —"

"Tony, I can't stand the pressure!" Jack tugged

at his beard. "Week after week the same thing! I'm getting too old for this sort of job."

"Thirty-four isn't very old," Tony said.

"I'm scared," Jack went on. "One of these days we won't pull it off. Then what?"

"OK, Jack, just calm down. We're in this together. You can't quit now. After we finish this one you can get out and find safe work."

Adam pulled back his hands and the ferns drew together. Noah was looking hard at him but he didn't dare speak. Adam knew what he was thinking, all right. He was thinking that what they had heard proved that those two men were murderers. But did it?

Noah nudged him and jerked his thumb over his shoulder.

Adam shook his head. They hadn't said one word about killing anyone. Just because Noah had got it in his head that they were talking about murder, he believed they were.

"I told my wife I'd be back at five," Tony's voice came to them.

Adam didn't think that murderers were married. He decided that they better hear something pretty definite before they went for the Coast Guard.

"This is the last time, I swear it," Jack said. "If I didn't need the money I wouldn't do it."

Noah was sure that now Adam would be convinced. He got ready to crawl away. Adam was beginning to feel uneasy. Maybe Noah was right. But if he was, they'd better be very careful.

"OK, Tony." Jack's voice again. "Let's get the coffee and get on with the plotting."

The boys flattened themselves behind the ferns as they heard the men, still talking, walk away in the direction of their canoe. Then they crawled quickly back across the pine-needle clearing. On the other side of it they stood up.

"Wait a minute," Adam said. "I see what you mean, but we didn't hear them say they were planning to kill anyone, did we?"

A strong puff of wind forced the branches of a tree down so that they swept the ground. A sharp shower of rain followed. As they heard the men crashing through the underbrush Adam dodged under the sheltering leaves, and after a few seconds Noah joined him.

In another minute they had climbed up the branches that grew close to the ground. As the wind swayed the leaves they saw Jack and Tony on the other side of the ridge of ferns.

"Hey, there's a beech tree," Tony said. "It should be almost dry under there. Come on, the coffee should still be hot."

Helpless, the boys watched the men trot across the clearing and sink down beneath them, with their backs against the trunk of the beech tree.

Tony reached into a bag and pulled out a thermos bottle. He poured two cups of coffee and drank some of his.

"Now," he said, "if we shoot Fred with the gun that can't be traced, we have to think of other ways of killing the two that are left."

"Coffee's good and hot." Jack passed his cup over for more. "It's a shame not to use the gun again. It would be a lot easier."

"Now look here, we agreed that we had to find different ways of getting rid of those three. That's the main point. It's harder to trace a murderer if he doesn't always use the same method," Tony said.

"How about rigging a car accident for Sam?"

"Well, it's possible. We'd have to find a lonely spot where there are no witnesses." Tony didn't sound as though he liked the idea.

Adam had been so shocked at the first remark about shooting Fred that he had trouble hearing what else was said. He tightened his grip on a branch and tried to breathe quietly.

Noah was not quite as surprised as Adam because he had been pretty sure about the two men. He mainly felt angry at Adam for not being willing to leave when they had a chance to escape.

"If you don't like a car accident, we could drown Sam," Jack suggested.

"How would we get him into a boat? Anyway, we used drowning once already." Tony found a box in the bag and pushed it toward Jack. "The trouble is, the Big Guy is too smart for a detective. He's smarter than we are."

"We could put all three on an island and let them starve to death." Jack dug into the box and brought out a doughnut.

"Not funny," Tony growled.

The men were silent for a few minutes and Noah watched Jack's hand. Noah's mouth had been so dry with fright that he hadn't been able to swallow. Now he felt his mouth watering at the sight of that fat, sugary doughnut.

Jack took a big bite, then stopped.

"Why did you get jelly ones?" he demanded. "That stuff tastes terrible!"

"Poison," said Tony. "We could poison Sam."

"Sure, I was just going to say that. Put poison in the jelly and no one would notice it!"

"Be serious, Jack. I can't stand your being funny at a time like this!"

"I am serious." Jack examined the doughnut. "I wonder how they get the jelly in these things?"

"I suppose they put it in when they make them."

"Look, I've got it!" Jack exclaimed. "We could give a doughnut a shot of poison with a doctor's needle." He pretended to shoot the doughnut with his finger. "It's perfect! No one ever thought of it before."

"Well, we'd have to get a hard-to-trace poison."

"You could ask your doctor friend about that," Jack said. "It's a great idea. All that sugar would cover up any little hole. Sam wouldn't suspect a thing."

Adam knew that the only chance they had was to stay perfectly quiet until the men below them left. He worried so much about doing this that he hardly heard what they were saying. He didn't dare to turn his head to look at Noah, but out of the corner of his eye he could see Noah's foot on one branch and his hand gripping another. Something one of the men had said reminded him of something.

"Well, poison for Sam. We might use a doughnut at that," Tony said. "Now what about Susy?"

"I'm not sure we need to bump off Susy." Jack finished his doughnut and reached for another one.

"Look here! We agreed that the three who knew about the first crime would have to go!"

"I like Susy. Maybe she didn't hear," Jack said.

"She was in the next room. She *had* to hear. Say, you've fallen for her."

"Well, Susy is cute and smart." Jack smiled.

"Sure she is, and she's got to go. I think maybe something bloody for her."

"No, not for her. I'd rather poison her, if we have to."

"Well, something gory for Sam, then," Tony

said. "Stab him? Push him down on an iron spike fence?"

Noah almost gave up hope then. He knew how Adam had fainted once when he had cut his finger. Adam couldn't even talk about blood. He watched in horror as Adam's hand clenched and unclenched on the branch in front of him.

"I suppose you'd like to cut off his head," Jack said.

Suddenly Adam's hand let go of the branch, his feet slipped off their perch, and he slid limply out of the tree.

Noah watched Adam fall to the ground, his head coming to rest with a thump on Jack's middle.

Jack let out a terrified yelp. Tony sprang up with a loud cry.

"What is it?" Jack yelled.

"A kid," Tony said in an awed voice. "A kid fell out of the tree. He must have been up there all the time."

"Get him off me," Jack demanded.

"He's knocked out." Tony bent over Adam.

Noah was far too surprised and scared to think. He just acted. He let go of his branch and dropped to the ground. Tony jumped and swore.

"Don't touch him!" Noah cried. "He's deaf. He didn't hear anything!"

Tony looked up into the tree. "How many more of you are there?" he asked.

"I'm — I'm deaf too," Noah said shakily.

Jack squirmed out from under Adam who still lay with his eyes closed.

"Look, kid, you didn't hear us plotting murders either, did you?" he asked Noah.

Noah shook his head.

"What's the matter with these two?" Tony asked. "Trying to scare us to death!"

"We scared *them*, that's what," Jack said. "They thought we were really plotting murders!" He walked toward Noah.

Noah looked up at Jack. He realized how tall Jack was when he stood next to him.

Seeing the look on Noah's face, Jack sat down.

"Look, kid, we're writers, see? We write for the TV show about the detective the Big Guy. Have you seen it?"

Noah nodded.

"Well, then, you know someone has to make up that stuff."

"They thought that we really were going to kill —?" Tony started to laugh.

"Shut up, Tony," Jack said. "This kid thought we were murderers and he came down to save his friend. *There's* a script for you."

"I saw 'The Big Guy' once," Noah said slowly. "My mother doesn't like me to watch it, though."

"She's right," Jack said. "I can't look at it my-self, sometimes."

Noah walked over to Adam, who seemed very peaceful with his eyes closed.

"He'll be all right. He just had the wind knocked out of him. He was lucky to land on me."

Adam stirred a little.

"Sh," Tony whispered. "Let's see what's the first thing he says. In movies it's always 'Where am I?' "

Adam's eyes fluttered, then opened wide. He looked right up at Noah. "The Big Guy! I know who he is!"

"Sure, he's the detective on TV," Noah said. "These guys just make up the stories!"

"I saw that show a couple of times when my father was out late." Adam sat up slowly.

"Fred and Sam and Susy aren't real at all!" Noah gave an uncertain laugh.

"I wish Susy was." Jack gave Adam a drink of coffee out of his cup. "You look a little pale, son."

"I think maybe he's hungry." Noah looked at the box of doughnuts.

Rain drummed hard on the leaves of the old beech and the four moved in close around the trunk. They shared the coffee and doughnuts. Jelly ones were Noah's favorite.

"I don't see how you think of all those stories and ways of bumping people off," Noah said, licking his fingers.

"After a year at this work it gets tough," Tony admitted. "You run out of ideas."

"If Sam or Fred were on the roof of a building," Adam said thoughtfully, "the killer could push him off."

"Adam, how could you!" Noah protested.

"Yes, but why would they be up there?" Tony asked.

"The killer could have pushed the wrong elevator button." Noah looked at Adam. "That's how!"

Tony got a notebook and pen out of his pocket. "Elevator. That's always good. Our killer could break the controls and let the elevator fall. That would do it."

"I'll never go to the dentist again." Noah helped himself to another doughnut.

"I guess you wouldn't want Susy in that elevator." Adam looked at Jack. "She'd be pretty smashed up."

"I'd rather get rid of her in a nicer way," Jack agreed.

"How about a horse?" Noah asked. "You could break your neck falling off a fast horse, I bet."

"Sure," said Adam. "The killer could be up a tree and throw something at the horse, and he'd take off, all right."

"I don't think Susy's the horsy type," Tony objected.

"But girls can ride as well as anybody." Adam looked at Jack. "She'd look great in real riding clothes — boots, fancy riding pants, and one of those black hats."

Jack laughed. "I think you've fallen for Susy too."

"He would if she had yellow hair," Noah said.

"Shut up, can't you?" Adam growled.

"You're a bloodthirsty pair," Tony said. "Any more ideas?"

"Adam doesn't like blood at all. That's why he fainted and fell out of the tree," Noah explained.

"Well, that's when I thought — you know. I didn't know you then. I don't mind scary stories."

"The trouble is —" Jack drained the last few drops of coffee into his cup — "Susy knows our murderer very well. She'd never let him get near her."

"Halloween!" both boys yelled together.

"These characters aren't trick-or-treat kids," Tony said.

"But the killer could be in a bunch of kids as a ghost or something," Adam said. "Then when he got near her she wouldn't know him."

"He could drag her into an alley and strangle her or stab her," Noah went on.

Jack shuddered.

Tony laughed. "Might not be a bad idea, at that," he said. "It would be a change from all the false mustaches and dark glasses and funny hats we've used."

The doughnut box was empty. Rain no longer sifted through the leaves overhead. Noah looked at his watch.

"Time for the tide change," he said, getting up.

"Thanks for the doughnuts and coffee." Adam stood up, too.

"Thanks for dropping in." Jack grinned at them.